Outlaw Queen

Outlaw Queen

By Dusty Richards

High Hill Press, USA

A Cactus Country Book

COPYRIGHT © Dusty Richards
High Hill Press December 2011
All rights reserved

Published by Cactus Country Publishing
A division of High Hill Press, USA

HighHillPress@aol.com
www.highhillpress.com
http://cactuscountrypublishing.blogspot.com/

Third High Hill edition: ISBN: 978-1-60653-051-1
10 9 8 7 6 5 4 3
Library of Congress Number in publication data

Cover Design by High Hill Art Department

This book belongs to the Frank Brother Series by western writer Dusty Richards. The original fictional story starts in the western Texas Hill Country. In the future you will meet the two young twin brothers, Lee and Grant Frank, who were orphaned by the murder of their mother and the suicidal death of their father during the Civil War in this same region of the Lone Star state. In future episodes, you will learn more about this pair of hard fisted young men and how they survived.

This portion of the series tells about their acquaintance, Rath Macon, who loses his great ranch in a bitter divorce to a fast spending social stepper of a wife and he must carve himself out a new way of life. A veteran cattle drover on the Chisholm Trail, after the loss of his own empire he plans to try to build another in the blue stem country of Kansas. *The Outlaw Queen* is the first book in the series.

Dusty Richards has won many awards in his career as a spinner of western yarns. In 2011, the Wild West Magazine listed him as the top living western writer. He won two Spurs, one for his novel *The Horse Creek Incident*. And a short story on Amazon, *Comanche Moon*. He also won the Will Rogers Medallion Award for the best western book in 2010 with *Texas Blood Feud*. The same year *The Sundown Chaser* won the prestigious Cowboy Hall of Fame and Museum Wrangler Award for best book. And his book *Wulf's Tracks* was a Spur finalist in 2011 and was a finalist in the Fictioneer Award.

Oklahoma Writer's Federation gave him two best books of the year Awards for *The Natural* and *The Trail to Ogallala*. The Cowboy Symposium recognized his service to helping others and his writing by awarding him The Writer of the Year Award. Dusty has also been inducted into the Arkansas Writers Hall of Fame.

You can find him at dustyrichards.com or dustyrichards@cox.net or you might just follow his tracks to the ranch house.

Dusty Richards
P O Box 6460
Springdale AR 72766

Dear Amigos

I want to dedicate this book to my good friends and publishers Lou and Bryan Turner of High Hill Press. In many phone conversations and long visits, we talked about the western and its demise in New York. Yet there are still lots of folks who enjoy western novels and short stories. Out of all our conversations came a new book division for High Hill dedicated to all things western. We're calling it Cactus Country. We didn't stamp a time period on it—but want to include every part of the frontier from yesterday to tomorrow. From the spotlight at bull riding and modern day rodeo to the rancher trying to make a living despite the anti-ranching efforts of uninformed organizations and government control. We want to take you back to the buckskin men who looked to the mountains from the eastern shores, and the brave souls who traveled west to seek their fortunes.

The west is a unique part of our history where men and women still say prayers and old glory still waves. Where men still tip their hats to ladies. Books are supposed to entertain and put you there—that's the purpose of Cactus Country. If it has a Cactus Country seal on it, you can count on it being a well written western.

And make sure to check out our anthology, *Cactus Country Volume I.* (soon Volume#2) It's a wonderful collection of western stories, articles, and poetry. Many of our authors have won Spur Awards, Heritage Awards, and Pulitzer nominations. Plus there are many future award winners included between its covers.

But now settle back and enjoy my novel, *Outlaw Queen.*

Dusty Richards

Chapter One

Rath Macon never wanted to hear the chant of another auctioneer, ever again. A sharp March wind swept the short stems of new oats in the forty acre fenced hay field. He felt surprised they hadn't let buyers and the hundreds of curious onlookers pull their wagons and rigs inside the stake and wire fenced acreage. They probably thought the fine spring crop would show how fertile the bottom land along Cedar Creek was to any prospective buyers. Those San Antonio bankers and their hired company, the Handover Auction Company, weren't going to miss getting a nickel out of everything in the court ordered sellout of the ranch.

Satisfied the cinch on his saddle was tight enough, he slapped down the stirrup skirt. All he owned in this world were three good horses. Stout red roans, two under packs saddles, held bedding, camp gear and supplies. He didn't have the faintest idea where he'd go next.

One auction team was up there selling what furniture and items were left inside the big two-story ranch house that stood to the north. Not much there. His ex-wife Vonita had taken the pick of what she wanted before she left in the fall. Another set of auctioneers were selling the remuda, teams, mules, harness rigs, farm machinery, shop equipment, brood mares with colts and his good stallions. He shook his head and prepared to mount up and leave.

"Rath. Rath, wait."

As he turned in the morning glare, a short blonde-headed woman in her twenties ran in and hugged him. Her openness shocked him and he blinked down at her. "Cynthia? Whatever is the matter?"

Tears clouded her blue eyes when she looked up at him. "I should of told you." She sniffed. "Maybe this would never have happened. It's my fault—all my fault."

With a shake of his head, he dismissed her concern and used a clean folded handkerchief to blot her wet eyes.

She nodded and took it in both hands to do it herself. "I wanted to telegraph you in Kansas—but I never did. I knew she was having an affair with him."

"That wasn't your job. I learned it soon enough when I got home."

"She never deserved you. Lots of—" She looked around and then walked him toward the horses for more privacy. "Lots of us married woman knew about her running around on you. He wasn't the first one either."

"She's got him now."

She nodded in defeat. "Rath, you've been done so wrong. I just hate to see you lose all this. You've worked too damn hard. It's a wonderful ranch and we all would love to have one like it."

"Well, this afternoon, some well-heeled guy with a pocket full of coins will take it off the hands of the First Texas Bank of San Antonio."

She squeezed her eyes shut and he comforted her shoulders. "I've got to be getting along. You tell Mike that I'll miss both of you at those Saturday night socials.

I had nothing when I came home from the war in '65. Guess I can do it over again somewhere else."

"Oh, Rath. God bless you. You helped us get started. But there's no way we can help you now. I just wish there was a way we could have done something."

He felt sad enough for the two of them when he stepped up in the saddle. She was too close for him to move the horse and he could see her big burly husband, Mike, coming towards them. Rath checked the gelding.

"Howdy, Rath. She's cried for a week about this deal and took on how we all should have helped you. It's a sorry kettle of fish, you losing this place. I told her there wasn't nothing we could of done."

"Mike, this is all my doing. She don't need to take no blame whatsoever. You have a wonderful wife and mother to your kids right there. Maybe when I'm out of here, she'll understand. No one could have seen this wreck coming."

He reined the big horse around the two and took up slack on the lead rope for the pack horses to follow him. He kept his eyes on the rolling cedar and live oak hills to the west. More than anything he needed to shut off that damn chanting—*what'll you bid?*

Headed in a jog out the back way—he didn't need any more *Cynthias* finding him. He carried a powerful enough sourness behind his tongue and it wouldn't take but a small jab in the ribs to make him cry. *Keep wetting your lips and focus on the direction where you're headed. And get the hell out of there.*

The even short lope of Red, the horse between his knees, made a smooth ride. It would quickly carry him far enough away so he wouldn't have to listen to the auction cries. And he wouldn't see the sad faces on the folks that came to witness the event. He needed no sympathy. His empire had been broken apart like a busted egg shell.

Near sundown he found a small rock-mortar tank fed by a spring and unloaded all his gear. No small task, but he might need some of it in his odyssey to hell or wherever he was headed. Coyotes didn't keep him awake, but they didn't lull him to sleep either. Dawn came and he washed his face in the tank, ate some jerky, and made a fire to boil coffee. His outfit loaded up again, he set out in the spring morning chill, this time headed north. On his previous cattle driving trips he had been looking for new range, somewhere beyond the Texas borders. The Comanche bands were still prowling the western parts of the Lone Star State and by himself he didn't want to become a target for some blood thirsty war party.

He eventually crossed the Red River on the ferry above Dennison north of Fort Worth. Already organized herds bound for the northern market were grazing in the southern reaches of the Indian Territory ready to head north. But the new grass was too short and had little strength. Places back off the main trail had enough old forage for the cattle to mix in with, but the ten mile strip of the main part of Jesse's Road, as many called it back then, was still too short to use.

So far he'd done a good job of avoiding folks that he knew. Maybe a rider or two recognized him, but he didn't want to go over all the things that put him in this fix. A wife leaving him for another man wasn't a big salute you told your real friends. Losing a big ranch like the TH—to a court ordered bank foreclosure didn't make a worthwhile conversation either.

The Indian Territory was dry country. That didn't stop the sale of alcohol. If a man wanted a drink or a bottle of fire water, a host of places dealt in it until one of Judge Parker's deputies smelled them out. They fined them on the spot or took them to Fort Smith for trial.

1871 had not been the greatest year in his life. His wife Vonita had been spending money faster than the federal presses made it. They'd been arguing about her acquisitions long before he had to take his last herd to Kansas. Art and the rest—she was furnishing the big house with French furniture and price had become no object. He had to stop her before he left because he was running out of money and that was the big blowup between them. If she'd been cheating on him before that day, he had no idea, nor did he even suspect it. But when he cut off everything except necessary food supplies and household servant wages. She became a ranting, screaming hellcat and left immediately for San Antonio to sulk and pout.

Rath couldn't go after her. If he had even considered it, the way was blocked by two thousand bawling cattle that waited on him to take them to market. He, his crew and the steers left the ranch two days later and his stomach never had another settled moment. Wires, letters, and threats followed him all along the way.

Someone said there were two dozen rivers to cross between South Texas and Abilene, Kansas. These water courses intersected the north-south cattle trail. In the spring of '71, they stayed swollen with flood water. That was the same time of year when men like Rath took their herds to the railroad yards at Abilene, Kansas. Several crossings that year were so much more swollen than usual by heavy rains in their watersheds. Despite all the efforts by his experienced crew to keep their heads above water, he lost cattle with each crossing.

Twice tornados sliced through his herd and the losses totaled near one-third of the original numbers of animals he drove out of Texas. At a time when he needed the most successful drive of his career, things went to hell in a hand basket. A softer beef market at the railhead added to his problems. So in the end he sat and drank hard whiskey in the Texas Saloon in Abilene, with the lawyer's papers from his wife Vonita stating that she was suing him for a divorce stacked on the water ring-scarred table in front of him. He never took another drink of hard liquor from that day forth.

In the twilight, almost a year later, he sat on the ground in Indian Territory with his back to the pannier, and studied the sparks popping out of the small pieces of dry wood he burned to make coffee. His hot brew revived his tongue with a twang and refreshed his mouth. Like a bronc horse turned out on the range, the harness and traces were gone. He had no wife, no ranch operation to hold him. He was free as a mustang.

Gratefully, he had no ties anywhere when he tried to go over his past mistakes. He enjoyed the leisure-like sipping of hot coffee while letting all the past anxiety drain out of him.

In the spring of 1865, as a bewildered young man, he had staggered home from fighting the weary battles in the muddy cotton fields of Mississippi with his fellow Texas Confederates and at last landed in sunny San Antonio. Those veterans bore nothing to show for their four years of service to a once almighty cause. All of them wore rags and were afoot. They'd foraged off the land to get back. There was no victory celebration waiting for them, no one was happy to see them but the tan-skinned dancers and waitresses who worked the cantinas. In the poor economic situation the country suffered, his co-veterans either turned into drunks or empire builders. He had chosen the latter path.

Mid-day in the cool early April wind, all hunched over in his jumper, he forded the shallow Wichita Crossing of the Arkansas River. He could see the two saloons and general store, plus some shotgun shacks on the north bank. Tired of his own sorry cooking he decided to buy himself a meal. The saloons were usually inhabited by worthless customers and hog farm whores, but he didn't fear either of them.

He hitched his horses at the rack, adjusted his holster out of habit and climbed the steps to the porch of the Texas Saloon. The batwing doors were tied open and rattled when he opened one side of the full double doors. Several hard hostile eyes turned to look at him and to appraise his entry. He ignored them and walked to the bar. A bartender dried his hands and came to where he stood.

"You need a drink?"

"No. You have a hot meal?"

"Beef stew and corn bread."

"I'll take that. And some coffee if it ain't too old."

"I've got some fresh. Where you want it?"

"A table on the side."

"She'll bring it," he said, pointing to a young girl. Coffee, too."

"Thanks."

"I never caught your name. Mine's Harry."

"Macon."

"Nice to meet you."

"Macon," a big bearded man said aloud and stood up by the stove. "I knew a man once named that. He owned a big ranch in Texas. He drove lots of cattle up here."

The man's followers around the stove laughed at his formality and scrapped their chairs around to watch the scene. The big man started for where Rath stood about to take a seat at an empty table.

"Well. Macon, what brings you up here so damned early?"

"I guess that's none of your business."

The big man stopped about twelve feet short. "Why that sounds kinda hostile to me. I was just aiming to be a little friendly with a fellow Texan."

"I know you." The man was a small time outlaw. "Your name is Costrow. I've seen the wanted posters. I don't need to talk to you. Go back to your pals."

"You threatening me?"

"Costrow! Leave him alone." Harry slid a sawed off shotgun onto the bar.

"Stay out of this, Harry." The big man made a casual wave and turned back to face Rath. "I asked you a question."

"You make one more step and you're dead." The muscles in Rath's left cheek twitched under the skin, his hand ready to answer.

Costrow showed some restrain and held out his hands. "I ain't going for no gun."

"Good." Rath met his gaze with narrowed eyes.

"Come on boys." The big man gave a head toss to the others. "We'll go keep warm and drink where they appreciate our business."

The three others got up and walked out the door looking pissed. They grumbled between themselves. Rath watched that they didn't get near his horses.

"Mister, I'm sorry," Harry said, with a wary shake of his head. "That bunch can get kinda bad. I don't like them any way. They're like buzzards. Besides they never spend any money."

Rath agreed. "Costrow's a two bit crook that Texas never missed. Thanks anyway."

"You get this stew?" the skinny girl he'd seen earlier asked. She held large bowl of steaming stew, a spoon and some corn bread on a plate.

"Yes, ma'am," Rath said. "Right over here."

The girl blushed. "I ain't no ma'am. My name's Claire. I'll get your coffee next."

"Sorry about that," Rath said.

"No need to be sorry, mister. They usually call me boy and that's worse."

They both laughed.

The stew proved to be delicious—it flooded his mouth with saliva. He blew on each spoon full and the corn bread was equally as good. The coffee tasted fresh. After his second bowl of stew and corn bread, he paid Harry and gave the girl ten cents. She beamed.

"You looking around up here?" Harry asked him.

"Yeah, there's some good grass country east of here. I plan to look it over while I'm up here."

"Good luck. Just watch out for Costrow."

"I'll be sure to do that."

Outside he stood on the porch, the country he wanted to see laid to the east. He felt a calling to the land of tall bluestem grass he'd discovered on earlier cattle drives. Too tough to plow, the farmers passed it by for smoother Kansas farm land west of there. The area had a lot more water in small streams and springs than Texas. It also boasted more winter, which meant cattlemen were in for haying cattle. But if a man got by that, there had to be money to be made. Good grass plus fattened cattle meant money.

Three days later, after he had been scouting around the small Kansas village of Cherrydale, he stopped to pick up some supplies. The general store was full of wives and daughters buying goods for the week ahead. Their men loafed on the porches and cast hard looks at the obvious Texan who had hitched his three stout roan horses at the rack. He felt their gazes following his every move, but not being wanted or on the run, he hoped his appearance didn't jar folks too much. This was sure not Confederate ground, and though the war had been over for seven years, blood still ran deep in many places.

He waited patiently behind a yellow bonnet wearing young woman for his turn with the clerk.

"Ar' yah from Texas?" a grandmother missing some teeth, clamped on a corn cob pipe and asked from beside him.

"Yes, ma'am."

"We almost went thar," she said. "But instead my dumb husband came up *cheer*."

"You don't like Kansas?"

She snuffed out her nose. "I don't like all these blue bloods think they know everything. You stay here long enough, you'll get to know 'em."

"Thanks, ma'am, I'll watch out for them."

Catching a whiff of the young woman's perfume, he kept his thoughts about the matter to himself. When she turned, she gave him a cool smile and excused herself for taking so long.

"No problem, ma'am. I have all day." He removed his weathered high crown hat and she perked up a little.

"Do you have a place near here?" she asked.

"No. But I'm looking for one. Thank you."

"Excuse me, my name is Mary Ann Cates. I would like to invite you to our weekly social and supper at the Highline School House this evening."

"What time?"

"People gather up there at five or so."

"What should I bring?"

She fell into a warm smile. "First time they'll let you off bringing anything."

"Miss Cates, thank you very much for the invite."

"I am Mrs. Cates. Sorry, I wasn't clear. But you are very welcome. I didn't catch your name?"

"Rath Macon."

"Rath, I hope to see you there this evening."

"I'll try to find it."

"Oh, anyone can show you the way."

She was gone in the rustle of a starched dress taking her slight perfume with her. Blue eyes, blonde, sweet mouth, he knew nothing except she said, "MRS." He guessed her age as twenty. But her invite might be a way to learn more about the region—damn, he could still smell twinges of that lavender scent.

Pipe chewing granny had edged by him with her order while he had conversed with Mary Ann. "Yeah got a wife or family, Macon?"

"No, ma'am."

She was waiting on the boy to bring her something to finish her order. "Well, you watch out for 'em. I'd hate to see a young man like you skinned alive."

"I'll be most careful. What was your name again?"

"Maude Grimes and I got three daughters ain't married either."

Someone laughed, which drew her scowl and she left hugging her poke of things.

His order quickly filled, he went out in the warming sun and began to put them away in a pannier on a pack hose.

A tall man in a buttoned up overcoat came over and spoke to him. Obviously, this man with a salt and pepper mustache and boss of the plains Stetson hat was no farmer. "Good day, sir. I see you're new up here in Kansas."

Rath's hand touched his gun belt out of habit— had he not seen a gun ordinance sign? The weapon was a part of him after the years of packing it.

"I'm sorry, am I breaking your laws."

"No, but most folks in eastern Kansas don't carry arms. We're peaceful folks and hope most gunslingers stay west of the line."

"I am not a gunslinger I can assure you." He pulled down the canvas cover on his pannier ready to re-tie the hitch and stopped to turn and shake the man's hand. "Rath Macon's my name."

"Herbert Cone. I'm the town law."

Rath nodded and turned back to tying the hitch over his pack. "What can I do for you?"

"You no doubt are here on business?"

"Yes, I am."

"Cattle business?"

Rath nodded. "That's my brand."

"Then I have a man wants to talk to you."

"Who's that?"

"Cherryville's banker, Silas McDonald. Never hurts to know a banker. He figured anyone had three good looking roan horses like yours had some sense."

Rath stole a look across the mud-rutted street at the bank building. First Bank of Kansas was a rather non-imposing looking building between a barber shop, who he also needed to meet, and a saddle repair shop.

"Never hurts." Rath finished up the hitch.

"Want to walk over and I'll introduce you to McDonald. You like this country?"

"Yes, I've been exploring it. Are my horses fine here for the moment?"

Cone nodded, looking impressed at his animals. "No one will bother them. Crime in Cherrydale is not much of a concern." Then he smiled. "Makes my job that much easier."

"Mr. McDonald, this here's Rath Macon, who owns those three roan horses we've been admiring," Cone said to the man behind the short fence inside the bank building.

McDonald, a man with lots of girth in a suit and tie, and bearing a long black beard, rose to his feet. "Good day, sir, let's adjourn to my real office."

His hand shake was firm for a soft-handed man and his eyes were like two hard chunks of coal. He showed Rath to a chair and thanked Cone for bringing him. "Close the door going out."

"Now," McDonald headed to a wooden swivel back chair behind the polished desk. "What brings you to Cherrydale?"

"Grass. Tall bluestem grass. I was here two years ago to look around, but this has been my first chance to come back and really look things over."

McDonald offered him a cigar. Rath refused pleasantly. Then the banker opened a drawer, produced a fancy bottle of liquor and two glasses. "How about a drink?"

"I don't drink. Thanks anyway."

"What about sporting women?"

"I guess I'd have to pass on them today, too."

The amused man leaned over his desk. "My gawd, man, what do you do for entertainment?"

"Look for ways to make money." His fingers tented, he slumped back in the leather chair. "I've rode over a few thousand acres around here the last few days. All grown up in winter cured tall blue stem. That grass could have raised tons of beef. Means this country has been under grazed and the land owners lost the sale of beef, bankers like you lost the interest and the bars and stores never sold much."

"Ah, you're a real economist."

"No, sir, I'm a Texas cow man. And any fourteen year old boy from my country could have told you that."

"Now where would these people get these cattle that you're talking about."

Rath's spider fingers did pushups in front of him. He never took his gaze away from the big man. "Do you have any idea what they sell for at the railhead?"

"Steer, big ones. Around ten cents a pound."

"That's right, if they ain't three years's or four's they don't want them. Takes them too long to get them fat in the Corn Belt. They don't want culls, cripples or cows either."

"So?"

"Every herd comes up the trail has several limpers, younger steers and cows in them. You know what they're worth up there?"

McDonald shook his head.

"Two dollars for their hides and they feed the rest to fatten hawgs. So the drover gets nothing. Like the sore-footed ones—buyers won't dare load them on the train. In sixty to ninety days up here on this soft ground, why they'll out run my roan horses."

McDonald never said a word like he was ruminating on Rath's every word, then he asked, "Can you buy them?"

"Yes for ten bucks a head. Of that money you pay me two."

"You said—"

"I don't want for us to be run out of business by cheap competition. Someone goes to figuring on it, they won't have the money to up your ante. Ten buck is too rich for them. I get two bucks of that for setting up the deal and hiring me some boys to help me get them put out on these places of yours."

"Mine?"

"Folks owe you money. How're you going to collect? There ain't going to be no booming crops for sale around here this fall. You issue a loan on each one for fifty bucks a head, delivered a year from now. They have to feed them hay next winter and keep them in good condition or we collect the cattle and put them out to someone else with no payment to abusers."

"How many head are you talking about?"

Rath looked him dead in the eye. "How deep are your pockets?"

"Why-why, I can see you making several thousand dollars out of my operation."

Rath never smiled at him. "Why don't you hope I make twenty thousand dollars?"

"If this is such a wild deal, why ain't you doing this yourself?"

"I'm not a banker. I'm a cattleman. You aren't a man to rope maverick cattle or throw steers from horseback. I can read a bad brand at a distance and know on sight every head of stock you'll own this year."

"Why for you to make ten thousand dollars— that's five thousand head of cattle at ten dollars a head. That comes to investing fifty thousand dollars."

"I asked how deep your pockets were?"

"What if they all die?"

"Guess we could go to California and buy a citrus grove." Rath sat back and wagged his head in disappointment at the man's question. Didn't he have any guts?

"You've got a plan to make that work, too?"

Rath shook his head matter-of-factly, to dismiss the man's concern. "Naw, I'm still working on that one."

McDonald laughed until his beard jerked. "You aren't funny Macon. I'm just sitting here and figuring how to find some tough Texas drovers and get a lower bid from them to do the same thing for half your price."

"You can do lots of things. But I have the experience at assembling cattle and how to market them."

"Where would you start acquiring these cattle?"

"Way ahead of them arriving here. Those trail bosses know how many of them culls there are in their herd. Two buck versus eight is a helluva of a markup. Plus they can argue all summer and those buyers ain't giving in and putting one of them culls on the train. Their customers will only pay for good cattle. Those other cattle have no market up here."

"Who handles all the business?' McDonald was settled back in his chair.

Rath felt his plan sounded better by the passing time to the man. A decision from the banker sounded closer. He doubted that McDonald had any person capable to run such an operation, even if he tried to cut him out of it.

"I don't handle the money. I'll get you the cattle and manage them, your people handle payments and settlements."

"What do you expect in the mean time?"

"Enough to cover my expenses until we settle. We'll settle after the whole operation is over."

McDonald nodded. "Who else did you try to sell this plan to?"

Rath shook his head. "You're number one. I've been up here before, but not really seen this much grass. Or, I'd probably been back sooner."

"If we had fencing—"

"There isn't much fence in Texas—yet."

"What do you do with the crazy ones?"

"Cull them at purchase or yoke them."

McDonald frowned. "Yoke them?"

"Hitch them to a slow one. They break fast that way."

McDonald laughed. "You Texans are unsinkable."

"No, we just handle things."

"What about yourself?"

"I was sued for divorce in Texas. The judge in Texas ordered my ranch to be sold to settle it while I was up here last year with a herd."

"What was the result?"

Rath shrugged. "I own those three horses and the clothes on my back,"

"What kind of a judge ordered you to sell your operation?"

"He's in the Texas justice system in Bexar County."

"You didn't seek a higher opinion?"

"My business was in collapse by then. I didn't feel hiring any more lawyers would be worth the effort. Besides she had spent all my money."

"Remind me not to move to Texas." McDonald looked reflective at his desk top. "I want some time to consider this operation. It sounds solid enough, but I'd need some partners in this deal."

"I'm not going anywhere for a while."

"Good. I own a property with a solid house you can use to live in until I decide what I want to do.

There's enough furniture to be livable. I'll see what I can do."

"Thanks. I'd accept your generous offer of a roof over my head."

McDonald rose and looked out the higher window. "If our deal folds, what will you do?"

"Try to find another partner. I think I can convince an individual or group to do this on some scale."

The banker shot a puzzled gaze at Rath, "How did you come up with such an idea?"

"You ever rode a horse from south Texas to Kansas?"

McDonald shook his head. "No, I haven't."

"Let me assure you, you'd have plenty of ideas by the time you got up here."

"I imagine I would." McDonald laughed and shook his head as if amazed. "Marshal Cone can show you the Flannery place. Make yourself at home out there. Looks like rain's coming."

"Thanks." A free roof and place to park his horses wouldn't be bad. Maybe he could find that school house social. *Mrs.? What was her name? Ah, Mrs. Cates.*

"Drop by in a few days," McDonald said as he showed Rath out of his office.

Rath surveyed the bank operation with teller windows and the five employees working on books and waiting on customers. Those rebel bank robbers running around in Missouri and Kansas had obviously not found this one yet. McDonald didn't look ready for them either.

Marshal Cone rode out with him to the Flannery place despite the threat of rain moving in. An easy acting guy for a lawman, he listened when Rath questioned him about what his defense would be against one of those gangs robbing the Cherrydale Bank.

"I watch close for signs," Cone said. "They usually send out scouts to look things over. I wondered at first about you when you rode in if you were sizing up the bank. Then I learned who you were from a guy you talked to about running cattle. Godfrey, you recall talking to him?"

"Yes. I talked to him one day on the road," Rath said. "He wanted to buy one of my horses."

"You ever decide to sell them you let me know."

Rath promised he would.

The Flannery place's pens looked solid. He unloaded his things inside the house as a light rain began to fall. Cone pitched into help him and then after they walked around the lot in the drizzle to be certain the roans would stay in, Rath turned his horses loose inside. They brought a pail of water from the well with them to the dwelling.

Inside the house, Rath built a fire in the stove. "How far away is the Highland School house?"

A slow smile crossed Cone's mouth as he sat on the ladder back chair. "You heading up there tonight?"

"I was invited."

"Maybe ten miles."

"I'd still have time to ride up there?"

"Plenty."

"Guess, I'll shave and then ride up there. If you'll give me an idea how to get there." He put a kettle of water on the wood stove and sat down at the wooden table across from the lawman.

Cone described the way to the school. When he finished the lawman started to excuse himself. "Need anything let me know."

"I will. If you ever figure that someone is sizing the bank up for robbery and need backup, send word. I'll back you."

"I will. Thanks."

Rath saw him to the door. He realized the quiet man was a lot more complex than he appeared at first. The lone figure under a slicker rode his bay horse down the lane headed back toward Cherrydale in the falling shower. Door shut behind him, the house was getting dark from the storm coming in, when he crossed the room to get a candle lit. This cobweb clad home would do for his usage for the time being.

Shaved and his hair brushed down, he went back out under his own slicker and saddled Red. He took a canvas sheet along to keep his saddle seat dry while he attended the event. He also knew from experience that these late spring storms could turn to snow. He'd been caught in some. The closer he drew to the school house, the more folks in farm wagons and buck boards headed the same way spoke to him as he passed. They seemed friendly and he felt an evening with these new people would be better than his own company had been for the past few weeks. He was ready to meet the folks in this new land.

He wondered about *Mrs. Cates*. Strange how one moment in the store she was single appearing and then she set him straight. Like, she'd forgotten she was married. Nice looking woman, too. But he wasn't on any search for another. His last choice had left a bad taste in his mouth. Sour enough that he'd not easily be taken in by some sweet smiling female.

The rain let up some when he found the school. There was a long picket rope stretched across the school house yard. "This a public hitch rack?" he asked a young man hitching a team of draft horses to the thick rope.

"Oh, yeah. Mister. It is. Hitch your pony here. These horses of our's ain't cranky."

He hitched Red and covered him with the canvas.

"Nice looking animal," the youth said, joining him on the way toward the front door.

"Thanks, he's a good horse. My name's Rath Macon."

"Tad Goulby's mine."

"Nice to meet you."

"Yes, sir." He ducked inside ahead of Rath, who saw no familiar faces in the welcoming throng of people standing inside the open lighted door way. Men were taking wet rain gear from the people coming inside and hanging them on wall pegs for the guests.

"My name is Trudy Green." A gray-headed woman stepped up and took his hand in both of her soft hands.

"Nice to meet you, Mrs. Green. Rath Macon. I'm new here." He removed his sodden hat and nodded to her.

"So nice you came by, sir. We'll hang your slicker and hat up. Have an interesting evening, Mr. Macon."

"I'm sure I will. Thank you." He gave both items to a gray-headed man who was about his height.

"We'll be eating shortly," the man said. "We've got some good cooks up here."

He nodded. Out of the blur of all the people looking and glancing at this new arrival, a familiar looking tall woman in a light blue dress crossed the floor—all smiles.

"I see you have taken my invite serious, Mister Macon."

"Yes, Mrs. Cates, I did."

"Mary Ann," she corrected him and took his right arm. "Come with me, there are people here you need to meet."

"Call me Rath then. Where's your husband?" He looked around for the man who she belonged to.

"Charles is dead."

He wanted to retract his wise remark. He would never—never have been a smart mouth about a dead man. "But you said—"

"I am Mrs. Charles Cates."

He met her blue eyes. "Excuse me?"

"Of course. I want you to meet Sam Ogden."

He shook hands with the friendly man, smiled and said how pleased he was to be there. She took him down the line introducing him to others and they ended up at the long table piled high with fabulous looking food.

"We'll say grace, then I want you to be my guest and fill your plate," she said under her breath. No time for him to decline, the prayer had begun. She was a real nice looking take charge female.

Chapter 2

How long since he had last danced? Mary Ann was a cloud for a dance partner, she moved with him like a soft breeze and he could hardly believe how much he remembered about dancing. They swirled around the room to polkas and smoothly two stepped to ballads. Waltz fiddle music had him back to work, boxing his boots around. The musicians took a break and she gave him some ice cold sugary lemonade. The high feeling they'd had since its inception at the end of food table slowly dissolved into reality.

"I must apologize for asking about your late husband. I simply thought when you said you were Mrs. that he was alive."

"A wonder you came, isn't it?"

"No, ma'am. I'd come anyway."

"I'm sorry I had to correct you. But I'm not Miss anybody."

"May I ask what happened to him?"

"You may ask." She lowered her voice. "He was shot and killed in Missouri riding with the James Gang two years ago."

Her words knifed him. He looked hard into her blue eyes for an answer. "My regrets."

"No need, the matter is over. I, of course, had no idea. I thought he was buying livestock for a firm out of Fort Scott. Obviously that was his front. I am Mrs. Cates. Or was anyhow. Some people believe I am still in touch with his gang." She turned, "Now if you would rather I—"

He cut her off with a finger to her lips. "I would much rather keep your company. A few weeks ago, my large Texas ranch was sold in a bank foreclosure auction because my ex-wife filed for divorce."

"And she won?"

"Obviously, she did. She is now my ex by Texas law."

"I'm so sorry. I don't know which of us has the tougher story to tell."

"You obviously do. Nothing you could have done about the life he chose. I simply let her go."

"No children?"

"No children. In your case?"

She shook her head. The music makers were back and it was polka time. In the two steps it took to find the beat of the music, they were off swirling around the room. He could see the wetness in her eyes as they whirled to the quickness of the song, but there was no need to stop. At last the dance was over and they were in the less populated portion of the room, she had her back to the crowd, facing the beaded-wood siding on the inside wall.

"Shame it's raining outside," he said. "Or we could go out there."

She nodded and used a handkerchief to blot her eyes. "Would you take me home in a little while?"

"If you know the way."

A smile crossed her mouth. "I do and I will be fine in a short while. I don't want to leave here looking upset and draw too much attention. I was past crying—once."

"If I—"

"You did nothing of the sort. You are a wonderful dancer and—there is not a single man in this room, that—who wants to dance with an outlaw's wife?"

"How old were you when you married him?"

"Nineteen. We were married for two years."

He stuck his bent finger to his upper lip. "I'm sorry. Was he local?"

"Yes, he'd gone off to war like the rest, came home and bought a place. I should have wondered how he could afford to do that. We began to date when I turned eighteen, and then we were married. He was gone a lot buying stock, he said. But we had two pleasant years.

"Then one day three Pinkerton men came to our farm and demanded I turn over the farm to them. They said it was bought with ill-gotten gains."

"What did you do?"

"I hired a lawyer and he had a judge make them stay off my place. But they camped at the gate.

"He never came home again after that. I received the newspaper clipping that said he'd been shot by lawmen in a surprise attack on one of their hideouts in Missouri.

"I also got a letter written from Cole Emery, who I suspected was one of the Younger Brothers. It had been posted in Springfield, Mo. He explained that Charles loved me and knew once that they had identified him as a gang member that they would wait for him to return here and that was why he never came back home. He went on to explain that he was buried in a Methodist cemetery and a local person had a stone placed on his grave, marking his name on it. That if I ever needed anything, I could reach him at an Indian Territory address."

"I didn't want to bring all that up."

She shrugged and completed dabbing her eyes with a small kerchief.

He wanted to hug her, but this was not the time or place. "This is a slow one. Let's dance. How many know about all this?"

"They don't know about the letter. I never shared that with anyone, but you. The rest is common gossip. They must think the gang comes by my place whenever they're in the area to see me."

"Gossip can be a bad thing."

"Especially when you're the widow of a famous outlaw."

"When it gets to be time to leave. You let me know."

A smile crossed her mouth and her eyes twinkled. "I'm having too much fun dancing with you. But we can leave in a short while."

They finally excused themselves and left. The rain had passed eastward, but more looked close by. He helped her into the buggy seat and drove her horse around to where Red was hitched. With the roan tied on back, he took her directions and they went down the road in a jig trot under the clearing night skies. He wasn't in that much of a hurry to get her home, but she said it was the gait the horse usually held for her. They reached her place and drove up to the white farm house in the starlight under some large trees. Their body heat under the throw made for a warm place on the seat.

He tied off the reins and put his arm over her shoulder. "Peaceful and quiet out here. Nice place."

She hushed the two excited collie and they minded her. Turned to face him, she asked, "Where were you at four years ago?"

"This time of year? Oh, getting ready to take cattle to Kansas. Why?"

"We could have met then."

"And changed our lives you mean?"

"Well, maybe."

"That don't count, Mary Ann. What really counts is what we do with the rest of our lives. We can't go back and walk that path." He used his hand to slice the world on towards her horse's rump. "We have to cut a new trail. You want in on the new one?"

"Can you see where it will go?"

He dropped down so his shoulder was against hers. "I'm making a deal with a banker here, Silas McDonald, to buy cull cattle and mend them with area farmers and all of us make some money."

"Rath Macon, anyone ever tell you that you're a schemer?"

"When I explained my deal, he asked if I was an economist."

"Really—"

She was right in his face and impulse forced him to kiss her on the mouth. Not a quick kiss and pull away—it was a long sweet one. And he couldn't recall how long it had been since he had kissed anyone—let alone anyone as sweet tasting as her. If he'd had wings he could have flown to the quarter moon over head.

They finally sat back to get some air in their starved lungs. It was something he felt would never happen to him again. But it had and he needed to think deep and hard about the repercussions to him and her both. He had nothing but three horses and a plan. He couldn't ask her for anything.

"Did I shock you?" she asked.

"No. It was me. I thought I'd used up my last chance at finding someone. Obviously I haven't. But we better put a little time in here. I'll put your horse up and go on home. This is too important to me to rush into something this serious."

"Can you come back and go to church with me tomorrow?"

"Let's hold onto that, too. My deal might not work here."

"You can't ruin my reputation. You might ruin yours."

He drew in a deep breath. "No. Give us some time to know how all this will work."

She sat up, sliced her right arm out and smiled. "You say the word and we'll go down that road as far as we can. Would you come in for some coffee?"

"No. Give me some time."

"You can have all you want. Put the harness on the shafts. Sugar goes in the pen beside the barn. He has water and hay there. I can go along—"

He shook his head. "I will see you."

"When?"

He grasped the words out of the air. "Monday night."

"For dinner or supper?"

"Supper."

"I'll kill a chicken. You like fried chicken?"

"Yes."

He backed out of the buggy and helped her down. A kiss on the cheek and he sent her toward the front door. *Lord, don't let her stop.*

In the starlight she stopped on the porch and waved. He nodded, then took the horse around and unhitched him. Sugar in the lot, he checked his own girth, then swung into the saddle. There was still a light on in the house. He considered stopping Red and going up there—but he thought better of it and rode on instead.

Damn, he tried to clear his head, the one who wasn't going to get involved with anyone. What did he go and do? Found Mrs. Charles Cates, the outlaw queen. No one would date or even as much as dance with her. Putting his heels to Red's side, he headed for the Flannery place.

He spent Sunday re-setting shoes on his three head. Took a sponge bath and shaved. Then he sat on the porch swing and rocked. Too much going on. Too much to worry and to wonder about. Had he been too sharp with her? Maybe he'd run her off. Was he too tough acting for McDonald to consider being in business with?

Should he have taken a drink with the man to seal the deal? No, he didn't drink any more. Was his deal too big for a small town banker? He closed his eyes to shut distractions out. Time would have to answer his questions. But could he wait for them to unroll? He swung harder in the seat, the rusty chain groaned.

He went to bed early. Grateful he fell asleep quickly, he woke before dawn made coffee and some breakfast. Only twelve hours to wait for a fried chicken supper. No reason that he had not gone to church with her—except he wasn't ready. Escorting the widow of an outlaw was no problem for him. Charlie had been sprouting daisies for two years—he wasn't coming back to challenge him.

Shortly after sun up, a man and a woman drove up in a farm wagon. They stopped at the yard gate. Rath knifed in his shirt tail and went out to see what they wanted.

"My name's Olaf Damon and this is my wife Shirley. We live next door and hope you stay here. We didn't get a chance to meet you at the dance, but we're going to town in the morning and thought if you needed anything we'd fetch it for you?"

"Right neighborly, thanks. I don't need anything, but I'll stop by and meet you again."

"You buying this place?"

He shook his head. "I'm just using it. McDonald said I could."

"Guess you want a big ranch, huh, coming from Texas and all."

Rath agreed. "Yes, that's what I'd like."

"This ain't a bad farm. Last fall, I asked him if I got time to put out some wheat on this place if I could farm it on the shares.

"He never told me I could till it was too late to plant it. Man don't know much about farming."

Rath agreed and smiled at Shirley. "Thanks for stopping by."

"You never asked him if he was married?" she complained as Olaf clucked to the horses to go.

"The *vey* that he danced with her all night I'm sure he's not. . . ." The rattle of the wagon cut out any more words that he could understand.

The *vey* . . . he meant the *way*, made him chuckle going back inside. There was some land he wanted to ride to north of there. He'd saddle Rusty and go see some more country. Rusty was a younger horse and needed riding the most of the three. He didn't expect the three-year-old to buck, but he might, especially if it was cooler.

McDonald didn't know it was too late for Olaf to plant wheat. He didn't know farming, he was a banker. My, my, he was learning things fast about this country. Rusty under the saddle acted up the first hundred feet, but he talked him out of it. However, an hour later a big prairie chicken shot out from some thick grass and the gelding lost it. He was a quarter mile down the road, getting him out of crow hoping and dancing around.

The episode made him feel good. At least he wasn't hiking back to the place walking after his horse. Ah, young horses were made to put you on your toes anyway. His heart settled down and he passed a neat homestead with several acres of winter wheat showing a green cast. There was also a plot of bottom land being plowed for corn planting. Spring was coming fast.

A loose herd of a half dozen work horses lifted up their shaggy heads at his passing. Surprised someone didn't have them up getting them in shape for the season. Who knew who they belonged to?

He sat and watched a nice stream, swollen with dingy water sweep under a wooden bridge and the water flooded a little into the edge of a field. Might get tough somewhere down stream to someone trying to get a herd across a larger river. He had lots of experience at that. It was never nice and those crossings never were warm except when going back home in the summer time.

He dropped off the high point and rode in from the back to the Cates place on a road used to service the fields. She had several acres of short wheat stems waving in the afternoon breeze. Three months from then she'd have a thrashing crew there to feed. Two collie cross dogs were barking at him

She came out on the back porch and her hand shaded her eyes against the bright sun to see him. Even at the distance he saw her excitement—he felt it too. And Rusty began single footing going downhill. Lord, even the horse knew something was up.

When he reached the yard, she joined him. He dismounted to walk with her and lead the horse to the pen. He felt different than after the dance. It was like they'd become strangers who had just met.

"Hush," she said and stilled the dogs' barking.

"You all right today?" he asked. He squatted down and made friends with them.

"Yes, you're early," she said. "The one with the black on his head is Scotty and Buster is the other one."

"Nice dogs," he said and stood up. "Am I too early?"

"No, no. I heard the dogs begin to bark, looked out the kitchen window and saw your horse. And I said, "He's here.""

"I was looking at some country and came by that way. Is that your wheat planted all over the hills?"

"Yes. Mr. Hansen farms for me."

"Have I met him?"

"I don't think so."

"Is this the original farm Cates bought?"

She nodded. "I came here as a bride and have lived here ever since. They said it might be dangerous, me living alone, but no one has ever bothered me. Guess they're afraid I still have some contacts with the gang and if they do anything to me, the gang will get revenge."

"One way to be left alone. I just can't imagine men shunning you."

"They have. I'm fine, maybe it turned out right and I was waiting for you to come save me."

He had turned up the stirrup over the seat to loosen the cinch in the barn alleyway. Out of the sun, it was cool in there and goose bumps ran up his arms under his sleeves. He dropped the stirrup and caught her by the shoulder. They kissed and he hugged her.

"This has been a lonely hill, hasn't it?"

Her face was buried in his shirt. "Yes. When you wouldn't stay—when you wouldn't go to church—I worried I'd seen the last of you. I'm so glad you're here."

When she did look up at him, her eyelashes were wet, but she was smiling through the diamond sparkles. She beamed. He hugged her waist to him. It was narrow and he could not believe why any man in his right mind hadn't stolen her away.

"I was afraid," he said turning back to the saddle.

"Really? Put it in the tac room," she said from behind him. "Then turn him in with Sugar. He can eat hay there and get a drink. Do I scare you now?"

"No. It wasn't you. It was me I was afraid of."

She nodded that she'd heard him and opened the tac room door.

He took the rig off, the pads in his arms and dumped the saddle on the horn in the neat's-foot oil smelling harness room. She latched the door when he backed out. Her hand looped easy-like on his elbow as they walked out into the sunshine. Warm sun rays soaked his skin and he patted her hand, then squeezed it.

"You have other help besides this Mr. Hansen?"

"Two neighborhood boys. They keep the weeds down, pick up things. They always need work and some money. Come with me, my tulips are about to bloom."

They admired the tall wax like bright buds in the back of the house. He noticed her well-fenced garden had been plowed and waited for more warm weather to be planted.

"Potatoes and peas are in the ground already."

Then she guided him to the back steps and up on the porch. She changed shoes to slippers in the hallway. Then he hung his jumper, hat and gun belt on the wall pegs. One look at her polished hardwood floors and he began to toe off his boots

"You don't have to take off your boots for my part."

"Oh, I'm not going to mar those floors," he said.

"You wouldn't. Besides they might become scars of—affection to me."

He hugged her shoulder and laughed. "Mary Ann, you are some woman."

She washed her hands at the hand pump in the sink and he followed suit.

"Handy, isn't it?" she asked.

"Your house is well fixed."

They went into the living room and she showed him a seat on the stuffed couch. Getting her dress bottom gathered, she sat down beside him. The room looked like a dollhouse to him, everything in place and neat looking. Even when Vonita had all her fancy furniture in the big house, she never made it look this good.

"It's early for supper," she said, snuggled under his arm.

He closed his eyes for a second. All he wanted to do was kiss her. What he'd thought about doing in the back of his mind ever since he saddled Rusty to ride over there. He'd fought it long enough. She turned and like some magnet drawing metal fillings, they kissed. He dropped off into a world of a spinning tornado. His mind centered on her.

The honey like taste from her lips, the fire of passion swirled his thoughts. He was being carried away.

When at last they had to breathe, he knew all his resistance was gone. Expired was the best word. Getting his bearings, he rose and went to the lace curtains and looked out at the greening land. He didn't look back.

"I didn't come to steal your virtue, Mary Ann. I'm a man myself in transition. I was once successful in business, but that's blown away. I feel I will find myself a new place in life, here in the bluestem or somewhere. But I can't promise you anything. I'm looking at a project that might be the first step."

He drew in his breath and hunched his shoulders. What else did he need to tell her?

"Be patient with me," she said and put her hand on his shoulder to join him. "I am not rich, but I do have this place and I am not stuck here if you must move on. I am not wanton. No man has been in this house, under this roof, since my husband was last here, save my farmer and some boys who I invited in to pay them for their work or fed them lunch."

He nodded that he'd heard her. "I'm not here to question you. I thought my wife and I would have kids and grow old together. But she had other plans, even I could not support—"

"Can you get over her?"

"I'm over her."

"Good. I think intuition is sometimes the best way to make your decisions. My intuition since I first met you was—"

"What?"

"If you weren't afraid of my past, I'd be your woman."

He laughed aloud. "Your past?"

"Yes."

"My heavens, do you think I fear Jesse James coming here and claiming you away?"

"There are many around here who still do?"

He took her in his arms and looked into her eyes. "I'm not afraid."

"Good, come with me," She took his hand and led him to a side door. When the two pane, wooden mill-made door swung open, he saw the sun shinning on the lovely handmade quilt of a double bed.

Inside, she closed the door behind them and he nodded.

Chapter 3

He left her place before the sun peeked up. She'd made him a large breakfast of fried eggs, ham, big biscuits and black berry jam. He felt full. He felt good about their relationship. However, when he rode out other things had popped in his mind. How was McDonald doing on his consideration about their deal? He'd go by and check on his horses first. Cox said crime was low in the country, but his roans were lots of temptation to steal. Both whined when he rode in and drew a smile. He noticed there was something tacked on his front door. Who left him a note?

He dismounted and went over to read it.

GO BACK TO TEXSAS

UR LAST WARMING.

Hell, they couldn't even spell. Who left him such a note? His first response was to shred it, but he stopped and folded it up. Cone might know something about who was behind it. No way he was going back to Texas. And no one was going to scare him into leaving this country. He better not let her know what they did. She was nervous enough that they might do something to him over their situation. That note tacked on his peeling paint door didn't come from Jesse James—it was local. Who wanted him out? He'd done nothing to anyone to make them pissed off that he could think about—besides stepping into the shunned outlaw queen's life.

Nothing inside the living room where he parked his panniers had been disturbed. He took his .44/40

Winchester out of the house, made certain it was loaded and jammed it in the scabbard. From there on he'd need to live with it. Were they serious? Must have been—who had he stepped on? No telling, but it might be on account of his interest in her.

He walked around the front yard, several horse prints were there and some narrow mule shoe tracks. Maybe a good thing he had been gone.

With a shake of his head, he mounted up and rode into town. He located Cone in the saddle shop. The lawman looked up from in the back, thanked the man for working on the horse collar and went to meet Rath in the front of the shop.

"Jim," Cone said over his shoulder. "Meet Rath Macon."

"Howdy," the man said and waved from his work bench in the back.

"You alright today?" Cone asked.

"Nice to meet you, Jim." Rath dropped his voice. "I found this nailed on my front door out there this morning." He handed him the folded paper from his jumper pocket.

"What is it?' Cone frowned at the writing. "You weren't home when they delivered it?"

"No." That was all he needed to know.

"Any tracks?"

"Yes, they sure didn't come alone."

"I wonder why they don't like you?" Cone herded him outside the bell ringing door onto the boardwalk. "Like did you piss in someone's soup?"

"No," Rath chuckled at the man's words. "I haven't done much of anything to make me a target that I know about."

"They damn sure can't spell, can they?"

"I like last warming."

"Can I keep this?"

"Sure, but don't show it to a teacher. They might make you do the third grade over again. Is McDonald in town?"

"Sure. I spoke to him this morning. I won't mettle in your business, but a few folks are worried about you. Do you know about Mrs. Cates' back ground?"

"Yes, she told me. She's the widow of a famous outlaw gang member."

"Yes. Lots of folks around here knew her husband. I guess he was raised around here."

"And?"

"Well, there has been word that the gang he belonged to looks out for her. I guess that's why most single men—most men have avoided her."

"I'm not worried about that. The ones left that note didn't ride with Jesse either I'd bet."

"No, he wouldn't leave any note." Cone chuckled. "You have business with McDonald today?"

"I'm going in and speak to him."

"Look me up when you get through. We can get a special lunch plate over at Minnie's Place.

"That's the café across the street?"

"Right."

Before he left Cone, he checked the sun time, it was near noon. He was still full from her breakfast, but he'd join the man anyway. The lawman was no fool and he knew lots about the workings of the country. Was he holding out suggesting who he suspected had left him the warning? Something told perhaps Cone knew more than he let on. This was his ground and a lawmen had to know lots of things happening under the surface.

McDonald was outside of his office reading something, standing up by someone's desk. "Ah, Macon good to see you. Come on back to my office."

They went in and he closed the frosted glass door behind himself. "What's new for you today?"

"Tulips are blooming."

"Spring must be here." The chair springs made a complaining sound when he sat down. "Learn any more about Kansas that will make us money."

"I appreciate the place to stay."

"That's nothing. I took that place in when the husband died and his wife went back to Missouri."

"My neighbor Olaf would like to farm it for you."

McDonald frowned about it. "I talked to him about it and he said I was too late."

"He meant to plant wheat this year."

"Well, you tell him to come see me. I just as well have him farm it."

"On another issue, before I got back to the house last night, some night riders must have come by. They tacked a note on the door. Go back to Texas. Your last warming."

"Who in the hell was that about?"

"They couldn't spell."

"Did you speak to Cone about that?"

"I did and he's looking into it."

The big man leaned back in his chair. "You must be a controversial person getting night raids."

"Or stepping on someone's toes, huh?"

McDonald leaned forward, in a low voice. "Who in the hell wanted you gone?"

"If I knew I'd walk up and slap them. so they'd have a reason."

The banker began to laugh. "I really believe that you would do that—just to see."

"You have much night riding going on around here?"

"We did back in the war days, but nothing I've heard about it recently. On the matter of our business, I have spoken to two men who may put in with us on this cattle deal. Both agreed that there might be some profit in doing that. They liked the sound of it and have said when I got the details to come back. That means explain it like you do."

"You need me to go over it with them?'

"Yes."

"I don't have a suit coat even, let alone a white shirt and tie."

McDonald agreed. "I can furnish that if or when it becomes necessary."

"Good. This must be men you can trust."

"I do or I'd not told them a thing about it or asked for their participation."

"In four weeks, the first cattle will be crossing the Arkansas River headed up here. I want set up down there to meet them. So by then we need to know how many head we can buy."

"That's where you're going to deal with the drovers?"

"That's my plan now. If I don't get run out of here."

McDonald dismissed that with a head shake. "We can handle that."

So they parted and he felt McDonald was in the deal and maybe more. The café came next. He found Cone seated at the end of the long counter talking to a hefty waitress.

"Marley, this is Rath Macon. New man in town from Texas."

"Howdy." She put on a big smile and stuck out her hand to shake. "Glad to meetcha'. What'cha need?"

"My pleasure, I'll have what he's eating."

"'Alright, two specials coming up."

Cone lowered his voice. "What did he think about the night riders?"

Rath shook his head. "Wondered who they were."

"I'll have some answers tomorrow."

"Good, if I knew them I'd go up and slap them in the face so they'd have something to complain about."

Cone chuckled and shook his head. "I bet you would."

"That's what McDonald said too."

"I'll have you an answer in the morning. They can't keep that down around here and someone will know about it and talk."

"Good. I can't imagine who I made mad being here."

The food for two bits was piled high on his plate. Shame, he wasn't even half way hungry for all she served them. Man, he'd given his eyeteeth for such a meal lots of times half starved and all alone. He also caught some small things about Cone and the blonde waitress when she checked on them and refilled their coffee mugs. Just small details shared between a man and woman. But there was a connection there more than just a waitress and customer. None of his concern anyway.

He parted with Cone promising him to be on the watch for anyone tracking him. Something that twenty-four hours ago, he'd not even thought about. So he left town on board Rusty and made a wide circle north at first. He felt like someone might be trailing him.

A few miles out, he reined off in some thick woods cover along a creek and set back in the brush cover to see who was behind him. Nothing came for a long while then a boy standing in the stirrups came through riding a tall dark mule. He was looking for someone or something.

"Hold up!" Rath ordered and the boy instantly laid forward on the mules' neck and went to beating him to run.

Rusty busted out after them and Rath undid a lariat. When the mule discovered a horse was tracking him, he sucked his tail against his butt and really went to running. The teenager in overalls was shouting and cussing for him to go faster. But Rusty thought it was a game and put on speed. The *reata* swooshed through the air and sailed around the rider's chest. With his right hand, Rath jerked the slack to cinch his catch and slowed Rusty down with his left hand on the reins. He didn't want his tracker to be jerked off the mule–yet.

"Who in the hell are you looking for?" Rath demanded when had him stopped.

"I was just–I mean."

"You want me to jerk you out of that saddle on your ass or are you going to tell me why you're on my back trail."

"I'm looking for a spotted heifer that got out."

"I don't believe that either. Now try your name."

"John Smith."

"That ain't your name." Rath started to back up Rusty. The rope grew tighter.

"No, don't." His eyes became the size of saucers at the action about to take place.

"Talk then and no more lies."

"My name's Willard Springer. I was paid to report on where you were going."

"Who paid you?"

"A man–no." He held out his hand as the rope tightened. "His name is Snowberry."

"What does he do?"

"Farms, I guess."

"Were you with those night riders last night at my place."

"No. No, I was home in bed."

"But you know them by name."

Springer shook his head, looking paler by the minute. "I don't know them. They all wear masks."

"I understand that in Kansas masked night riders can be sentenced to five years in prison at hard work." He was making that up, but he wanted the boy scared.

"I—I don't do that."

"I want you to go into Cherrydale and tell Marshal Cone this whole story. If you don't I'm filing a criminal warrant out for your arrest for night riding."

"What will he do about it? "

"I'm not sure if you come clean, he might let you off if this is your first offense."

"I ain't never been any trouble in my entire life. Well, 'sides watermelon stealing."

"You report right now to him and tell him what you were doing with me and the night riders."

"I never rode—"

Rath shouted at him. "Are you listening to me?"

"Yes. sir, I am and I'll do just that."

"If you don't do it like I say, expect to be held in the courthouse for trial."

"I won't do nothing, but what you said to do."

"Take the rope off and ride like the wind to town."

"I'm going. I'm going."

He sat Rusty watching the boy and his shaggy coated mule head for town. Coiling up his *reata*, he tied it back on the saddle. Who was Snowberry? Why did he want him out of Kansas? Maybe it was an old war sore festering. That was fought all over again, even seven years after Lee surrendered.

All he wanted was to find a job or make one that would earn him enough to climb back in this world. Scrambling was no fun. He didn't consider himself a patient farmer. And if you couldn't do it from horseback he didn't like it.

By late afternoon, he was back at Mary Ann's. The dogs acted friendlier and even Sugar whined at Rusty. She came wearing a straw hat the wind threatened. Obviously from her dress, she'd been planting in her garden.

"Well, you caught me in my working clothes."

He shook his head. "You look good enough to me in anything, don't worry about it."

They kissed long and slow. It brought back lots of memories about her from the night before. He had a bad case on her. Lucky for him that they considered her the bandit queen—she'd saved all her sweetness simply for him.

"You have not changed your mind and decided I am not who you want?"

He made a face at her words. "Why of course not."

"But I need to warn you about what I'm going to do."

Her blue eyes wide open, she looked hard at him. "What's that?"

"In a month, I'm going to have to move down on the Arkansas River and meet the cattle herds, if my plans proceed. I may from then on be real busy down there setting up purchases."

"Can I go along with you?"

"Now how would that look?" He took off his hat and beat his leg with it.

"I really don't care."

"I do. That's the answer. You can say 'I do' to a preacher."

She narrowed her blue eyes. "I didn't tell you that you had to marry me."

"Maybe I should have asked then. Mrs. Cates, will you marry me?"

She looked about to cry then she blurted out, "No. But Mary Ann will."

"Good. How big a deal do we need?"

"Not much."

"There isn't much in my account. Do you want to do it in your church or at the Saturday night social?"

She narrowed her eyes at his request. "You'd do it there?"

"I'm not afraid."

"The social. Can we wait two weeks?"

"That's fine."

"Oh, Rath that is so sweet. You've made me the happiest girl in the world. I don't want you to think I tricked you. You don't owe me. I was blind as you were last night. That was not blackmail, was it?"

"No. Not blackmail. We wanted that union and now we'll make it permanent."

"Do you have anyone to invite?" she asked.

"No, they're all in Texas or on the trail. What about your parents? You've never mentioned them."

"They have never forgiven me for eloping with Charles because they knew he was a southerner."

He shook his head. "They may really hate you marrying a Texan."

"I will invite them." She took his hand, began to sing, *Roll Out the Barrel* and they began polkaing around the yard. The dogs went to barking at their dancing and the two of them finally fell down on the ground laughing. She leaned over and he kissed her.

"I can already tell," he said. "We're going to have a fun life together. The outlaw queen and the ex-reb from Texas."

"Yes, yes, a fun time."

"On a serious note, some night riders left a note on my door last night. They couldn't spell, but said for me to go back to Texas and this was my last warming."

"Warming?"

"They couldn't spell warning. I showed it to Marshal Cone in town. He's doing some checking. It's no problem. A whole army couldn't keep me away from you."

She jumped up and pulled him to his feet. "I may be kinda bold, but I think we need to go practice for our honeymoon."

A woman after his own heart, he looked down at her and laughed. Then he swept her up in his arms. "We need to do that right now."

"Put me down," she protested. When he wouldn't stop carrying her, she clutched his face between her hands and kissed him hard. He figured she'd never known much about having fun, but she had turned out to be a good spirit. In two weeks, he'd have a new wife. One he could laugh with—looking back he and Vonita never laughed like this. It was all serious, all kind of made up and it had to be fancy and served well or she was upset. Mary Ann was a damn sight freer.

Chapter 4

It rained on Thursday afternoon and he went back to the Flannery farm to check on his horses and told her he'd be back in the morning. They had a hard time parting and when he reached the other place, it was past dark. The rain had quit. He put Rusty in the lot and decided he'd ride out on one of the other horses in the morning. A wind came in behind the storm and the temperature dropped. He built a fire in the fireplace to drive out the cool dampness, spread his bedroll out on the floor, and took off his boots. He decided to sleep in his britches and shirt, not knowing how low the temperature might drop that night. He had brought the Winchester inside with him.

The sound of mules and horses drumming around the house woke him. His heart pounded in his throat. On his bare feet, he looked out the windows at the milling raiders carrying lighted pitch torches. They wore pillow case hoods with eyes holes cut in them.

"Come out here, you gawdamn rebel outlaw! Get your ass out here or we're going to burn this gawdamn house down!" More cussing and a mule had a kicking-squealing fit that made the other horses and riders angry.

Most of the men he could make out carried old shotguns. A few balanced rifles on their knees as they milled around. He sure didn't want to face buckshot head on either. He'd have to keep low.

"Hold your fire!" he shouted.

Things quieted down. He added, "I don't know what you want, but come back in the daylight like men and we'll discuss it."

"Where's that sumbitch at?" someone shouted.

"Shut up," someone else said.

"I've got a loaded repeating rifle in here and two pistols. How many of you want to die out there. Raise your hands so I can count them."

More cussing.

"When this starts it won't be easy dying," Rath shouted. He inched back under the kitchen table and closed his eyes. Ricocheting buck shot might be his worst enemy.

The first blast took out a living room window with shattering glass and that was followed by several more windows being blasted and more whiskey fed cussing. Most of those old scatter guns looked like the muzzle loaded kind. So they only had one shot. He raised up and took three hard swift shots out the broken open front window with the .44/40 at the torch bearing ones in the front then dropped behind the kitchen wall. By his count, he got two men and one horse or mule. But it scattered the riders. They had not expected his reply with the rifle hitting anyone.

"Get out of here!" was the cry from a leader and a thundering retreat followed.

He could hear an animal's deep breathing, obviously in pain. Six gun in his fist, he slipped out the back door and listened to retreating hoof beats. He couldn't see anyone in the thin starlight. The animal in pain wasn't in the front yard, it was over in the lot. He opened the gate and two of his spooked roans shifted around. The third was on his side on the ground. One of those bastards had shot Rusty. He used a pistol shot to end the animals suffering. Best he could tell the others were unscathed. Back out of the pen, he went with the cocked .44 n his fist to where a still mule laid on his side in the yard.

"Get him off me," a man pinned under the animal asked.

"I wouldn't piss on you if you were on fire," Rath said. Two more men lay silent by their smoldering torches.

"My leg's killing me."

"What's your name?" He paused considering what to do.

"Eddie Perry."

"Why in the hell did you do this to me?"

"You were a reb soldier, right?"

"Yes, but that damn war's been over for seven years."

"We heard you rode with Bloody Bill Anderson."

"Who told you that? I wasn't with Bloody Bill Anderson? You dumb ass, I fought in Mississippi mud the whole damn war."

"You going to get me out?"

"You going to bring my good roan horse back to life that you shot."

"I never shot him. How could I have do that?"

"That's your answer."

Sick to his stomach over his loss, he rode into Cherrydale at dawn and found the lights were on in the diner. At the counter, Cone got up looking shocked when he came inside.

"What in the hell's wrong?' the lawman asked, seeing him not wearing his hat and his face blackened by gun powder smoke.

"They came back. Shot one of my good young horses. I killed a few of them. They shot out the windows in the house. I was on the floor. They said I rode with Bill Anderson."

"That's crazy. How many are dead?"

"Two-three. You better get someone to board up the house. They shot every window out of it."

"I'll get a wagon and some blankets. And I'll get a few men to help me. You have any names?"

"Eddie Perry. He's the only one that was alive. He was still pinned under a mule in the yard."

"You shoot him?"

He warily shook his head. "I should have."

"You want some breakfast?"

"No, I can't eat. I'm going up to Mary Ann's and clean up. She may fear I'm dead."

"Mr. McDonald wanted to see you today. I was going out and find you."

"Send him word that I'll be back later."

"Damn night riders. That boy came and told me what he knew. You really scared him. He needed that. Then I warned a bunch of them the law was going to come down hard on them. They wouldn't listen to me, I guess."

"I now know why they shot at me, but wounding my good roan horse so I had to put him away was chicken shit."

"I agree. You go on up Mary Ann's place and I'll catch you there."

"I don't know what this will do to her. We've been planning on getting married. See you later."

Cone nodded.

Rath went across the street and bought a new shirt and pair of britches in the mercantile. He came out and swung in the saddle. Then he rode to Mary Ann's. Oh, Kansas had few crimes. Peaceful country, they told him. He'd never been in over two shoot outs during his entire life in Texas.

She rushed out of the house, no doubt upset seeing him hatless. "Whatever is wrong?"

He dropped heavily out of the saddle and hugged her. "Everything. Night riders came and shot out the windows of that house down there. Then one of them shot Rusty." He kept shaking his head, biting his lip to keep from crying.

"Sit down on the steps. Why Rath, you're really shaken. Did they wound you?"

"No. But I got a few of them. Marshal Cone's going after the bodies. I guess I should go over there and help. One of them said I rode with Bloody Bill Anderson. Hell, I was with muddy Bill in Mississippi."

"You look sotty. Are you certain you weren't hit?"

"I'm fine. It's all that black powder they shot at me. I bought some new clothes in town."

"Lets get you a bath then before you go back. Is the other horse alright?"

"He's fine." Rath stood up. "I'm sorry. I didn't want to ruin all your plans."

"Shoot, all I worry about is you being alright. We can make new plans."

"No, our plans are still on. Those crazy idiots thought I rode with Bloody Bill."

She nodded, gently guiding him in the kitchen. "You need a bath and we'll have to heat some water."

"Yes, ma'am."

After his bath and shave, he dressed in the new clothes and she nodded her approval. "All you need is your hat. Why don't you go get your things and move in with me now. I don't care what anyone says. Beside we'll be married in less than two weeks."

He agreed with a nod. "Someone is supposed to board the house up. It would be a little drafty. First I want to tell McDonald about the damage and see if we are going on with the cattle deal."

"Good, Can I make a suggestion?"

"Sure. What is it?"

"Why don't you go buy a new hat to get married in."

"Alright." A quick hug of her shoulder and he left for town.

A concerned looking McDonald met him at the front door of the bank. "You alright, Rath?"

"I'm fine. Is Cone back?"

"No, but I sent him more help." He herded Rath back to his office. "Were they crazy?"

"Someone told them I rode with Bloody Bill up here. I was in Mississippi for the biggest part of the war."

McDonald made a grave head shake. "There's still lots of anger stored up."

Rath agreed. "I thought about that on the floor when they shot out the windows."

"You're just lucky to be alive." He closed the door and turned back. Then he made his swivel chair groan sitting down and Rath took the chair before the desk "Is this going to scare you off?"

"I don't scare that easy. How about you?"

"No. I have found some firm partners. I believe we can start it. We may be limited some by how many we can buy."

"What will be the limit?" Rath listened close for the man's answer

"Oh, three thousand head. But that's lots of cattle."

"It's a start. When can we set up?"

"Whenever you're ready."

"I'm getting married in two weeks. I want to spend a week with her, then I'll go down on the Arkansas and set up."

"Who are you marrying?"

"Mrs. Charles Cates."

McDonald nodded and looked at him with a questioning frown.

"I know all about her background. I believe she's been wrongly shunned. Makes no difference, I have no connection to those outlaws. Nor does she."

McDonald nodded slow like. "Gossip is a cruel thing."

"It is. My marriage will not interfere. Let's get back to the things we need to do. I need to hire some drovers. We can't contain them without men on horseback."

"Can you find good ones?"

"They're up here or will come when I ask them. We'll need sixty saddle horses to start. A chuck wagon, cook and supplies."

"How many and how much payroll?"

"We can hire the riders for twenty-five a month. Three foremen to head up operations will cost forty a month apiece. I am going to set up some outfits down there to bunch them. Many limpers will be healed in a few months rest with big weight gains, we can sell them this summer. Those will be easy herded. The young cattle and cows will be what we can put out to farmers."

"How will you figure on the mix of cattle you buy?"

"I think we'll have two yearlings or cows to the one limper. That's my guess."

"So we can sell some of them off by fall?"

"Right. Limping cattle I think will have a quick turnaround. I have to buy cattle that simply limp, not with broken bones or badly damaged hooves."

"What will happen to them you don't buy?"

He shrugged. "They can feed them to hogs."

"Good. So you are going to inspect them."

"Me or one of my men. How we buy them will be the success of our business."

McDonald rubbed his hands together. "I'm anxious to get this on." He reached over and shook Rath's hand. "Start lining it up. Oh, and when is the wedding?"

"A week from next Saturday night at the High Land School House Social."

Both men stood and McDonald clapped him on the shoulder. "I'm pleased to be your partner. I'm sorry about their attack on you. Glad you came out unscathed. Cone will round them up. He's on your side."

"Good man. Thanks, I'll start hiring my help."

"The horses and wagon?"

"There's plenty sitting around up at Abilene. They'll be cheap."

"Good."

He bought a new gray Stetson in the general store with a silk wrapped brim and band. It had a factory pinched crown and he figured in a few rains he'd have the brim shaped to suit him. He tried to think of something he could buy for Mary Ann, but try as he did, nothing came to his mind. Outside in the sunshine, several people stopped him and they apologized for the nightriders and what they did.

He stopped and looked in a millinery shop window across from the bank. The lady in there was measuring a customer for a dress. He removed his new hat and stepped inside.

The shop lady stopped her work and welcomed him. "What may I do for you today, sir?"

"I'm going to get married in ten days. If I brought her in here could you make her a dress?"

"Oh, two days before would be enough."

"Who are you marrying?" the gray headed customer asked.

"Mary Ann Cates, ma'am."

"The out—."

"Yes, ma'am. The widow of the outlaw Charlie Cates."

"I didn't mean anything. It slipped out."

"I know. But she's been hurt by that kind of gossip. I hope when she's my wife that folks'll try to be a little more respectful."

"Oh, yes."

"I'll bring her by in plenty of time," he said to the lady who ran the shop. "Good day."

He was a little bitter over the woman's words, but they'd show her and any other doubters. He and Mary Ann would have a respectable life together. He unhitched his horse and started to ride out.

Cone came down the street driving a wagon with several men riding beside him. He reined up. "Only one's dead. The other two will live to stand trial."

"They sure shot up the house, didn't they?" Rath shook his head over the mess they made.

"It's a damn wonder they didn't hit you. I have some men boarding the place up." Cone shook his head. "Seems like no one can recall who told them that you rode with Bloody Bill."

Rath nodded. "I didn't figure you could get that out of them. A week from Saturday night, Mary Ann and I will be married at the school house."

Cone smiled. "I'll be there. Good luck."

He nodded and several others showed their concern as they rode on by with the wagonload of two wounded and one dead night rider. She'd be worried if he was gone for too long, but he needed to get Red and his things over to their place.

It was mid-afternoon when he rode into her yard with his outfit. The extra packsaddle was on top of the load. He had all his personal items in the two panniers hung on Rebel, the middle horse. The dogs came to greet him.

"Good to see you," he said, stepping off his horse and hugging her. His attachment to her ran deep, a whiff of some faint perfume and her willowy body in his arms recharged him. If one good thing happened to him since Texas it was surely her becoming a part of him.

"How did it go? I really like your new hat."

He took it off and showed her. "I also have real news. We're going to get in the cull buying business."

"Good. What do you have to do?"

"Oh." He kissed her. "Hire some help, buy a chuck wagon, find a cook, and locate some saddle horses."

"Is that all?"

He laughed. "That's all for now." She was sure sweet to hug and rock. He felt like a new man.

The tale of Cone's arrests and body recovery, he saved for inside. She about cried, but he could tell she grimly understood. Maybe this whole nightrider thing would be over after all this—but he saw no end to the tunnel until they found the leader.

Chapter 5

The ride up to the town of Newton took him a long day in the saddle. Somewhere either in Newton or up the road to Abilene, there were some things he needed. A chuck wagon in useable condition, and a team of mules to haul it. There were lots of those rigs never went back to Texas. The man had no one to drive them back and after they made the cattle sale the crew scattered. Many abandoned their wagons or they sold it to someone. The mules to pull it didn't need to be fancy, he was probably going to park it near the main herd and leave it there for the rest of the year. He'd kissed Mary Ann goodbye and pulling himself away from her was like leaving a meal starved, but he rode out on Red and leading Rebel who carried his bachelor camping/cooking things.

Not an easy separation, but what he needed to set up and quickly. He short loped the horses northward. In a few hours he observed they were started building the new leg of the railroad down toward Wichita. That would be the new railroad loading point next year so the farm folks around Newton could live without hell raising cowboys. They hated all the fury of being a cow town and it was common knowledge the Newton city council was paying for half the cost of the bond for the railroad to extend its tracks ten more miles further south.

Late afternoon, he spotted the yellow canvas covered bows of a rig beside a farm setup. He turned up the lane and rode up to the soddy. A hard-eyed woman in her thirties came to the door in a dress way too large for her and used her hand to shade the sun.

"What'cha need?"

"Is that wagon any good?" He nodded toward it.

"Why?" she asked in a whiny voice

"I may want to buy it."

"Look for yourself then."

He nodded, stepped off Red and dropped the reins. He left the two horses to climb over the board fence into the pen. The wagon had some brands on the sideboards. None he knew. Two half grown shouts in the pen woke up, grunted in shock at their discovery of him and ran away in a circle.

"Stupid damn pigs," she said under her breath, holding up the too big of a dress by the waist so she didn't step on the hem and fall.

The wagon looked solid enough. He shook the wheels to be sure they were sturdy, the spokes appeared to be tight and the iron rims on well. He figured once out of the pig pen, part of the smell would wash off. The tailgate worked and the dusty back cabinets needed a good bath. The canvas top would eventually need to be replaced. The wagon box was made out of boards cut from a cottonwood log. Probably would work. No water barrels, but it had a good tongue, double tree and singles trees to hitch to.

"How much you want for it?" he asked her not looking aside.

"My husband ain't here."

"What does he want for it?"

"How should I know?"

"You can't sell it?"

"I never said that."

"Whatever. I'd give you twenty dollars for it delivered to Wichita Crossing."

"How'd I get it there?" She looked cross at him.

"Haul it down there with a team."

"Too far." She shook her head. "Besides he took the team with him."

"Then draw it out by the road and I'll haul it down there."

"What will yeah give for it out there?"

"Ten dollars."

"What would you give for it in this pen?"

"Five dollars."

"Sold." She held out a long calloused hand for the money.

"What will your husband say about that?"

"I don't give a damn, pay me." Her palm was still out there for the money. Now she let loose of the waist of the dress that sagged below her hip line and the bottom piled up around her feet.

He looked at her hard. "I better not come back here to get it and him have a fit that you sold it."

She shook her head. "He won't do that."

"Why won't he?"

"'Cause he done run off with my sister."

"Huh?"

"I told you. He done run off with my sister and he won't come back."

Amused, he asked, "That dress belong to her?"

Her eyes mad enough to burn him down, she nodded.

He gave her ten dollars for the wagon.

"I don't have any change for that."

"Keep the rest you'll need it. I'll either find a team or send one of my men after it in the next two weeks."

"Who'll he be?"

"I don't know I haven't hired him yet."

"Seems to me you've got lots of unanswered things, mister."

"Rath Macon's my name."

"Darling Stone and I'm looking for a man."

"I'm taken."

She nodded like she knew. "I'll find one."

He started back for his horses. "Anyone got a team of draft horses or mules for sale."

She shook her head like she didn't know of any, and carrying the bottom half of the dress up so her clod hopper shoes didn't catch on the hem. "Wrong time of the year to buy them. Every one that has any needs them."

In the saddle, he agreed, saluted her. "I'll be coming after it."

"I'll be here too."

On to Newton, wondering about the excuse for the too-big-dress she had worn. Something was wrong. Maybe it was because of her sister-husband's disappearance. Maybe it was something else. He'd probably never know.

In Newton he met a farmer leading a team of horses wearing harness down the street. They been wintered poorly and were thin. He stopped the man and asked about the team.

"I'd sell them, I run out of hay a while back. I need to sell them to buy some corn seed."

"How much you want for them?" He bailed off Red and began checking their teeth and feeling their shins for splints. Young horses. Sound, too. The man wasn't lying, but he'd about starved them to death.

"I'd take twenty bucks for them and five for the harness."

"How about twenty for the whole thing?"

"You drive a hard bargain. Alright I'll take that."

Rath shook his head. The man didn't know how hard a bargain he could make. Now he had bought a chuck wagon that stunk like hogs and two horses so poor they could hardly stand up. Some good grass pasture or hay and they'd fill out fast. But what could he do about all that. Bargains had become expensive.

He headed back south with his new purchases. When he stopped at the woman's house again, she came outside in a wash-worn dress that fit her thin body much better. "What now?"

"I'm going to pull that wagon out of the pig pen with my horse. I want it washed with lye soap and water."

"Who's going to do that?"

"I'm hiring you to do that."

"What's it pay?"

"Ten dollars."

"What else have I got to do to earn that?"

"You have plenty of grass on this place. These two horses have been starved. Can you get them fed up? We only have two weeks."

"That's not much time." She winched the corners of her thin lips in distrust. "You buy some grain, I'll feed them. I'll hobble them 'cause there ain't anything going to get fat running around."

"You need hobbles?"

She shook her head. "I been thinking since you rode out. You need a cook for this outfit?"

"You know one?"

"Me. I can feed an army. I know. I know. Lots of cowboys don't like a female in camp, but I won't mess with 'em. I'm tough enough and the food will be clean and good." She spoke with a finality to her words.

"Wagon first. Let's get it out so you can get it cleaned and it'll smell less like pigs."

He rode Red into the pen when she opened the panel gate. When she didn't close it, he frowned at her. "Won't those pigs run off?"

She shook her head "Naw, I can get them back in with a can of grain. Go ahead and undo that lariat. I can hang it on the end of the pole and watch how it steers when you try to pull it out."

"Red can get it out," he promised her.

The rope hooked on the tongue and Red dug in when he felt the weight. The wagon needed rocked out of the ruts. Darling was busy directing the operation and soon it rolled out. She had him circle it around toward her house. "It'll be slicker than a gut when you come back in a few days. I've got some harness oil to use on that, too. If I make it all shine, will you consider me for the cook job?"

Amused, he sat in the saddle and coiled up his lariat. "You'll have to move down to the Arkansas River to be the cook. That'll be our headquarters."

"Won't bother me to move." She shook her head. "Did you ever figure out that damn dress business I had on when you rode up yesterday?"

"No, what was it?" He was about to laugh.

"My sister bought that dress to cut it down to fit her. She'd left it here when she ran off with him. I was trying it on to see what I could do with it to make it fit me when you stopped here. No chance to change when you rode up. So I just wore it."

Smiling, he dismounted and began to take the harness off the thin horses.

"I can do that. You ain't hiring no sissy. Just leave that harness here. And I'll have all my clothes to fit too if you'll hire me as the cook."

"You have some grain I can buy for the horses?" he asked, shaking his head in amusement.

She went over and caught his sleeve. "Yes, I do. And I am serious I want to be your camp cook."

"Down there?"

"Wherever you need this wagon parked."

"I'll send you word where and when I need you."

She made a frown at him. "You going to bring another team?"

"If they aren't strong enough by then. Yes."

She shook her head in disbelief. "No way they'll ever get that fat by then. What's the job pay a month?"

"Thirty dollars."

She wiped her hand on her hip then stuck it out. They shook and he said, "You've got the job."

He rode on back to Newton and arrived there about sundown. He ate supper in the Longhorn Bar's Tent with Ira Handby, a drover he knew. They had some tough cooked beef with mashed potatoes and soda biscuits.

"Tell me more about your deal." Ira asked.

"The cattle one?"

"Yeah that one. I also want to meet that woman you're going to marry too."

He'd told him about Mary Ann and his plans. He continued, "My job is to buy sound culls. Things the buyers won't take. I plan to buy them for eight bucks a head."

"Then you're going to graze them and when they're well, sell them?"

Rath nodded. "They've been culling them for two dollars and the buyer's been feeding them to hogs. I'm going to pay eight, graze them. I need three foremen to run three crews."

"How will it work?"

"Cattle that limp, we'll herd out on the open prairie. Most of them, if they have feed and water will heal quick and can be sold by fall."

"I know that can be handled."

"The young steers that buyers don't want, we can let some farmers winter them and get them big enough to sell next year. Cows we can bunch up. We'll find a market for them to stock new ranges."

"Sounds good."

"Pays forty a month. We need to form three outfits to handle the different phases in the next few weeks."

"You figured all this out?" Ira asked, shaking his head as if impressed.

"I had lots of time riding up here by myself."

"I bet you did. You've lost the whole TH—ranch and all that?"

"That's a long story. My ex-wife forced that on me while I was up here in Kansas last year."

Ira whistled. "I was up there at that ranch when you were building it. That's a dirty shame."

Rath nodded. "Spilt milk. You can't sop it up. I'll be more careful next time."

"How long is this job good for?"

"Should last a year."

"Count me in."

"Good. Think about two more men with foreman qualities."

"We can find two more, there's lots of good men up here."

"Then we need three crews. I found a chuck wagon we may need to work on some and a gal to cook."

"She tough?" Ira frowned at him.

"Tough enough."

"I ain't against a woman, but they got to be— tougher than any man."

"I think she can be. We'll give her a chance."

Ira nodded.

Plans were for Ira to find four good hands to start with and meet him at Wichita at the end of his honeymoon week. Harry in the Texas Saloon could point the way to his new headquarters, wherever he settled on. Four men would be enough until they got to buying. The burly man shook his hand and Rath went to find a place to sleep

Frank Walters found him on the streets of Newton before he left. "Words out you need a foreman."

Rath looked at the tall man with white side burns. *How old was he?* "What have you been doing?"

"I drove cattle up here three times. I can run a crew of cowboys."

"What have you been doing this year?"

"I rode up to Nebraska last fall after the drive. Got me a good dose of cold last winter and decided they couldn't give me enough of that country for me to stay up there. So I didn't get a herd to drive up here this year."

Rath went over his needs and the program. "You interested?"

"I've got to have work. When do we start?"

"Ten days I figure. Who's got a remuda up here? I need about forty sound head to start."

"Joe Thompson."

"How much will he want for them?"

Walters smiled. "You can buy 40 for ten bucks a head. Can I have the job?"

"Sound ponies?"

"All Texas mustangs. He thought he'd get rich selling them. He needs money now."

"Can you hire a couple of cowboys and drive them down to Wichita. I'll pay you twenty to keep them boys fed until my cook and rig's moved down there."

"That's no hard deal. What you pay them?"

"Twenty-five a month."

"Where can Thompson get his money?"

"Cherrydale Bank will pay for them with a note from me."

Walters nodded at him looking impressed. "You're damn serious, ain't you?"

"Damned serious. You may draw some trouble down there. There's some trash hanging around those whore houses and saloons. Don't mess with them. I'll back you."

In pencil, he wrote the forty horse deal out for McDonald. Then he wrote another for the Wichita store if he needed some supplies before he got down there.

"Here's the paper work. There is an X on the horse deal. The other should get you some credit at the store." He'd put the X on the horse deal so if Walters couldn't read he could act like he could anyway.

"Thanks, I'll make you a hand," Walters looked at the X and nodded as he pocketed the two papers.

So with that much done, Rath decided things were taking place. He lacked the third foreman and some more cowboys, but he'd not advertised for them until he was closer. There were lots of them up there. Maybe those two men could handle it and save the cost of the third one. He'd see how it worked.

Instead of camping he headed back for Mary Ann's place. It was long past midnight getting back. She and the dogs came on the run in the starlight to the barn with a lamp where he'd dismounted.

"How did you do?" she asked out of breath

"Good. Got lots done." He kissed her. "Anything happen here?"

"Yes, your old neighbor was by. Olaf?"

"What did he want?"

"He said there are five loose draft horses in the neighborhood down there that are cutting up and stomping the wheat fields. They've been out foxing men who try to catch them. They're also cutting up wheat fields. They want to hire you to catch them."

"Who do they belong to?" He took the saddle off Red and carried it to the tac room.

"No one knows. You can have them. But why would you want them?"

"I could re-break them and sell them."

"I never thought about that. You know about them?"

He nodded. "I've seen them before. I wondered why those draft horses are running around loose?"

"When will you have time to go get them?"

"Can you ride?"

"Sure, but I'm not a Texas cowboy." She blushed.

"You can ride Red and help me herd them. We can get them tomorrow."

"I'm game."

He put the horse up and with his arm on her shoulder they headed for the house. Before they reached the back porch, he already had plans for the horses. They might have to pull Darling's chuck wagon with them.

"You haven't had any trouble have you?" he asked her on the back steps.

"No. Why?"

"I just wondered." He closed the door behind them and shed his boots at the back door

She fixed him some bread and cold meat. "How did your trip go?"

"Good. Things went smooth, and I have two foremen hired and a cook."

"Oh, you got lots done. I missed you."

"I missed you too."

He felt settled to be back with her. Maybe things in his life would slow down. No nightriders here—so far.

They turned in right after he finished eating.

Saddled by the first glimpse of dawn, they were set to go horse hunting. He put her on Red and was satisfied that she could ride him. He swung onto Rebel and they headed back toward his former residence to find the loose ones. She looked very sure of herself with Red. They met a farm wagon and he stopped them. A man and a boy sat on the seat.

"Have you seen some loose draft horses this morning?"

The driver spit tobacco off the side and nodded. "Back a mile of so they were in a wheat field grazing. They yours?"

"No, we're going to try to round them up."

He spat again. "Yeah, they're a big nuisance. Several folks have chased them. They're foxy. Wish you two luck." The teenage boy beside him nodded.

"Thanks," Rath said and they rode on.

"He saw them?" she asked, riding in close.

He nodded. "A mile up."

The sun warmed quickly. He considered shedding his jumper but was too busy looking for the stray horses. They topped a rise and he caught sight of something brown in a distant greening wheat field. It was them. He pointed.

"I wonder who they belong too," she asked as she located them.

"Your guess would be better than mine."

"Let's cut across this open country." He led the way and she rode beside him.

"I really like your horse. He's the best one I've ridden since I was a little girl."

"He'll do what you want him to do."

She agreed. "Did you raise him?"

He nodded. They were from his own stallions and mares he had spent considerable time and money locating good breeding stock. Of course it all went in the sale. No crying over that, but it did kick him in the guts to think about his losses.

"I'm sorry," she said, obviously realizing talking about it hurt him. "I know how much that loss stabs you."

He showed her a smiling face and shook his head. "I'm near over it."

The band of horses threw up their heads at their approach. Suspicious and wary looking, they drifted to the south. She indicated she'd go west of them.

"Good, just go easy."

She agreed and made Red trot. Her standing in the stirrups warmed him more. She sure knew how to ride.

The loose horses trotted off at their approach, but did not panic. He hoped that they could drive them into someone's lot or pen. Roping them was his next plan, but that would only split them up. These five had an association with each other that made them into a band. He wanted to use that notion to his advantage. They weren't crazy mustangs. From the obvious white collar scars, they showed they'd once been harnessed. He wasn't upset with their movements so far.

They left the field and jumped a small ditch, then went east on the road. He waved that she was alright. They needed a lane that led to a farmhouse. It would happen, he felt sure. Riding side-by-side, the band had slowed to a walk. The big bay mare who he decided led them, kept looking back.

She was the cagy one, the rest followed her lead. The wind made her short mane stand up and when she turned back to the front, she shook her head in disapproval of their pursuit.

"Look." She pointed at two men running from their plowing teams to cut them off.

"They may head them in toward that fenced lane," he said, pleased.

The band turned and fled toward the farm house and buildings on the fence lined drive.

"Thanks," Rath told the men when the two of them reached the lane.

"They can't get out less they come by you," the farmer said, standing with his boy who from his looks was no doubt his son.

"Is there a lot open up there?"

"Sure is. I'm sure glad that you're getting them. We've tried to trap them. We didn't have any good horses like you two've got."

"My name's Rath Macon. This is Mary Ann."

"I know her. Glad to meet you, Macon. I'm Clyde. This is my boy Arthur. We'll help you catch them. Fact we'd do about anything to get them off this end of Kansas."

"Thanks again."

The pair walked with them up the lane.

"You settling around here?" Clyde asked.

"I hope to."

"Having a real stockman around here might be handy. These loose horses have been a pain for over a year around here."

"You need anything, come by her place. We'll be getting married in another week."

"Good luck to both of you."

"We may need it."

The horses in the lot and the gate closed, he shook their hands for the help. The two went back to their plowing. His young wife Neddy joined them and she talked to Mary Ann.

He undid his lariat and prepared to catch his first one. In the lot, they moved to the far end and he carried the loop in one hand as he scouted them. When he got close, they broke and he put the loop over the bay mare's head. When he leaned back, dug his heels in, she slid to a stop on the taunt rope. He came forward. She blew rollers out her nose, but when he patted her on the neck and talked softly she settled down some.

He led her over and Neddy offered him some lead ropes and halters. "You can bring them back, my man is sure proud that you're catching them."

With a nod, he thanked her and accepted the offer of halters, since he didn't have enough lariats to take them home.

Mary Ann was standing on the fence when he hitched the mare to the fence. "She wasn't wild as I thought she'd be."

Rath shook his head to dismiss any concern. "They've all been broke."

"Neddy asked us to stay for lunch?"

"Tell her we'll stay."

"Good," Mary Ann said, making certain the woman wasn't in hearing. "She's not afraid of the outlaw queen."

He chuckled finished tying up his first catch. She joined him in the lot and headed them back when they threatened to break. He roped them one at a time. After a little head tossing, they each settled down. When he got them haltered, she took the lead and tied them by the mare. Soon all five were hitched. He hugged her shoulder.

"That went well. She's waving for us to come on to lunch. The men are coming in with their teams."

"Let's go eat lunch." Her arm around him, she beamed. "I was a tomboy growing up."

He undid the gate to let them out. "I saw that today."

"It doesn't turn you off?"

"Heavens, no, girl. This is a partnership we're getting into."

She kissed his cheek. "Good. I can't change much."

"Don't."

Over the meal, Mary Ann invited them to their wedding. The three of them agreed to attend and acted excited to be invited. After the meal, they hitched the horses in line and he took the lead. She followed in drag and they rode for her place. Their arrival in late afternoon had gone without a hitch. The horses loose in her lot, he felt much more relaxed.

She was busy making supper and him relaxing in a chair, when Marshal Cone arrived. When Rath heard the horse coming he got up and wondered seeing the marshal in the saddle, what was wrong?

He met him in the yard.

"How are things going?" he asked the law man.

"I hate to bother you, but I think someone is here casing the bank. They showed up today. Do you have the time to back me, just in case."

"What did they look like?"

"Cattle buyers. Wore long canvas coats, expensive hats and were well armed."

"Do you need me to come in tonight?" Rath asked him. He was probably right, there were few cattle to buy in the area.

"I hated to bother you, but I have a strong notion you were my best bet, if they are with the James Gang or part of it."

"I can ride in tonight or come at dawn."

"Dawn will be good enough. I've asked two others to help us."

"Have some supper. She's about has it fixed."

"I better—"

"Come on, you need to eat."

"Alright. I sure appreciate you joining us."

"No problem." He showed him to the back door.

"Marshal Cone, how are you?" she asked, putting the food on the table. "I set you a place."

"Good," Rath said and winked at her. "I'm going in real early tomorrow. He's suspicious about some strangers in town."

"Oh."

"It may be nothing," Cone said to her.

"I guess you two can handle it."

"We'll give it a try," Rath said and after they washed up, they took seats at her table.

"You have a lovely place here," Cone said as they passed around the bowls of food.

"Thanks."

He nodded and smiled. "I hope you two do good together."

"We will," Rath promised him. "The two of us caught up five loose draft horses been cutting up wheat fields around here for some time."

"That will make a lot of happy people. I had more questions about them. No one knows who they belong to."

'I'm going to advertise and claim them if no one shows up."

Cone frowned at him. "Are they any good?"

"That's strange. They all five are solid acting draft animals, aren't they?"

"They really are," she agreed and excused herself to get the coffee pot.

That night the two of them laying in bed, talked about the bank robbery deal he was going on.

"Cone trusts you a lot," she said.

"I guess so. I hope that they are just what they say they are—cattle buyers."

"Oh, I do too."

"But he can't take a chance."

"Oh, I know. I can get the neighbor boys to harness and see how those horses will work while you're doing that?"

"Good idea. What will they cost?"

"Oh, fifty cents a day. They do lots of work for me."

"Hire them for a couple of days and see what they can do with them. This business I'm in on in town should be over in a few days."

She rolled over and kissed him. "I sure hope so."

He did too, taking her in his arms. He couldn't believe she really was his. He closed his eyes and savored their intimate closeness. They'd both had enough hell in their lives and deserved each other.

Chapter 6

Rath sat in a chair facing the front window of the millenary. His rifle out of sight on the floor beside him. He had a perfect view of the bank's front door and the lace curtain hid him unless someone cupped their hands against the glass to peer in.

Mrs. Brown who owned the shop had twice brought him some coffee. A pleasant lady in her forties, she asked him if he thought those men in town would try to rob the bank.

"I'm not certain, but it is better to be prepared than let them do it."

"Oh, certainly. Have you done law work before?"

"Not like this."

"You act so at ease. I'd be pacing the floor if I was in your boots—" Someone came in the shop. Mrs. Brown went to wait on her.

He re-crossed his legs. Being edgy wouldn't help. In a few days if they didn't try to rob the bank the strangers would move on. One of Cone's other men named John Towers, he met earlier, was acting like he was working in the main store as a janitor. Sweeping the floor and standing close to the front windows for a view of the street and bank.

On the roof of the saloon acting like a roofer, Alan Phillips was the other men in on the scout for Cone. Phillips was close to thirty by his estimate. The clock ticked slow. Noon time, a boy brought him a sandwich made of fresh rye bread and sliced corned beef with mustard. The tasty meal hit the spot where

Mary Ann's oatmeal had filled at home earlier. Traffic went by. Then when Mrs. Brown's clock chimed two pm, two men in long tail canvas coats rode up, dismounted in front of the bank. They tried not be obvious, but he watched them take in the street scene before they stepped up on the boardwalk. They pulled up their bandannas as they went inside. The robbery was on.

Rath reached over and picked up his rifle. A bank robbery was going down. When he stood up, she came with coffee for him.

"Oh, I'm sorry," she said, obviously seeing the intensity on his face when he excused her and moved to the front door to open it. Backed away from the opening so they couldn't see him in the shadows. He dried his hand on his pants and then re-gripped the rifle's stock. There was a cartridge in the chamber.

"Are they robbing it?" she whispered, huddled out of sight.

"I'm sure they are."

"Oh, I hope you aren't shot."

So did he. Then he saw a third man come up the street on horseback. Not a farmer, but he might be a look out for the robbers. He carried a pistol in his hand and tried to conceal it. But the six gun was way too obvious.

The door of the bank opened. A masked man started out. The horseback rider in the street began to fire shots in the air. Phillips on the roof cut him down. The rider pitched head first off the horse. Rath wanted both men out of the bank before he opened fire. The man in the doorway shot at Phillips—Rath shot the outlaw in the chest and spilled him backward. A second man firing a handgun in the air came out of the bank with a sack in his left hand, started to step over the downed one's body. His chest in Rath's sights, he shot him. Cut down by the bullet, he crumbled face forward on the boardwalk and shot his six gun at the feet of their horses who broke loose in a panic.

Rath busted out in the street looking, reloading the lever action rifle and looking for more outlaws. A hundred feet down the street, a rider took some wild pistol shots that shattered two plate glass windows, then whirled his horse to a run. Obviously he was part of the gang. He cut the horse down and the rider went off over his head,

John Thomas ran out of the mercantile store. "I'll get him."

Rath agreed and crossed to join Cone who had drug the two outlaws off the boardwalk to lay them out on the dirt. Phillips was off the roof and out of breath when joined them.

"Damn good shooting," he said to Rath.

"You did well," Rath said to Phillips.

The man shook his head. "Got lucky."

"I was on this side and afraid I'd hit someone if I did shoot," Cone said.

"That's why we spread out," Rath said. Sure wasn't Cone's fault and that was why he put him over there in the dress shop to cover the bank's front door.

Thomas came down the street with the last outlaw by the collar. A groggy looking man in his thirties who wasn't all there. "Here's the last one," Thomas said.

Cone handcuffed and made him sit on the ground. McDonald appeared in the doorway, white as a sheet. "No one's hurt in here."

"The money is in that bag." Rath indicated the flour sack on the ground.

A teller quickly swept it up and took it back inside.

Cone shook their hands. "Thanks, I knew I had picked the right men to help me. The town owes all of you their thanks."

"All of you ride with Jessie James?" Rath asked the sullen prisoner.

"Gawdanmn right, we did. Yes, and all of you will feel the edge of his anger when he learns what you did to his gang members."

Cone supervising the loading of the three dead men in a buck board, he came back and kicked the outlaw in the gut with his boot toe and doubled him over. "Shut up about Jessie James. He better not show up here either."

"Gentlemen," McDonald said from the door way. "All of you come in the bank. I have some good whiskey and I want to make a toast. You too, Macon."

He had a glass of grape juice for Rath. The rest were filled from the cut glass decanter. A toast was made to Cherrydale and glasses clinked. Then McDonald made some more toasts to other deals. Glasses clinked again.

They all shook hands. McDonald announced a twenty-five dollar reward would be made to each of them. Rath nodded. "Cone, if you can handle it I'll be going back to her place."

"I think it's over. Hope so. We sure appreciated your help." Hand shakes all around, he went after Red. It was sundown before he came up the lane to her house.

The dogs and her came on the run.

"Did they try to rob the bank?" she asked, after kissing him when he hit the ground.

"Yes, they did. Three of them are dead."

"Anyone I know hurt?"

"No. All were members of James Gang according to the live one."

"Did you know who they were?"

He shook his head and swung the saddle off. She opened the tac room door for him.

"Oh, your draft horses will work. Those two neighbor boys Truman and Ferrell drove them all over this afternoon."

"Good. I need to go get my chuck wagon and get it filled with supplies and get some water barrels mounted on them."

She hung on his arm headed for the back door. "Can we do that tomorrow?"

He laughed and tousled her hair. "Yes, it can wait that long."

"Good."

He closed his eyes inside the back door for a moment to remove his boots. Things in his life could go a lot easier. He needed to sample the honey tree. Yes, he needed to do that. He recalled again those angry looks on those two outlaws coming from the bank. The savage set to their faces like everyone one else was less than them. *Get out of our way.*

And then they were cut down by hot lead and they were nothing.

Chapter 7

He woke before sunup in the bed with his arm thrown over her. So he didn't wake her, he removed his it carefully. But to his regret, she stirred. "Not leaving without me."

"I was going to let you sleep."

In the dark room with only starlight coming in the window, he saw her wrinkle her nose at him.

"I wouldn't leave you."

They kissed, then he swung up and sat on the edge of the bed. She joined him and rubbed his shoulders. Her actions made him realize how tight his muscles were back there.

"What's your plans for today?" she whispered.

"Oh, harness a team. Go over to Darling's and bring that wagon into town. I need a couple water barrels mounted on the side. Plus the supplies loaded in it."

She laughed, busy dressing. "Will she have that dress cut down?"

"I hope so. You'll have to meet her. I think she's tough enough to handle a big crew."

"You said she told you that her husband left with her sister?"

He chuckled. "You can ask her about that. I wouldn't touch it for a hundred dollars."

"See you're the nice guy, that's what you are. Pancakes alright for breakfast? "

"Wonderful."

"See I told you so. I'd said, mud pies, you'd agreed." She laughed at her teasing.

"I would not have said, wonderful."

They both laughed.

"By the way, I want you fitted for your wedding dress at the dress shop."

"That will cost you."

"I can borrow the money. My reward from the bank robbery try may even pay for it."

"Alright I will go have the dress made."

"Last women I had would have had three made and worn something else."

"Aren't you glad that's not me?"

"I thank the good Lord every morning." He squeezed her shoulder.

In the kitchen, her busy mixing batter in a big crock bowl, she stopped. "I never talked to you about me."

"What part is that?" The serious look on her face warned him, she had something important to tell him.

"Charlie and I never had a baby. We were seriously married for some time. You marry me you may never have any children. I guess I held that back till now figuring that might sour our deal."

"It won't. I'll take you like you are."

"Good. Some men wouldn't."

"Some men wouldn't do anything."

She went off to pour her batter on the hot skillet.

"Are your folks going to hate me, since I'm a reb, too."

She purse her lips side ways. "I've not worried about them since I said I-do-to Charlie."

"You don't think we can mend that fence between you and them."

She turned the pancakes with a spatula. "Should I?"

"I lost my folks while I was off in the war. But if they were alive I'd sure be at least friends."

"I'll let you see what I mean."

"Hey, we don't have to do anything."

"Yes, you will be the nice guy." She delivered his pancakes, butter and blackberry jam. "I forgot to make syrup."

"This is fine. You jam will do."

"Yeah, nice guy."

The boys showed up early and he went out to meet them. Truman and Ferrell McEntosh. The two brothers acted a little nervous and barely shook his hand.

"Mary Ann tells me you boys've been working hard for her."

They both nodded.

"Guess the pay helps out."

They nodded.

"Well, she's going to need you this summer too. I'll be busy down in Wichita working cattle. So I guess you two will have plenty of work here."

"Ah, Mister Macon, we have to do some work on our family farm, too," Truman said looking for backing from his younger brother, who agreed.

"My name is Rath, I understand that. Tomorrow I need one of you to go with me and get a chuck wagon I bought and drive it back over here."

"I can go," Truman said.

"Today, let's shape those big horses hooves. They look cracked and chipped. I don't think they need shod up here in this soft ground."

"No, shaping them should do it," Truman said. "Will we be back by dark tomorrow."

"I sure hope so." The boys had relaxed some when she came out.

"I'm sorry. Have you three met?"

"Yes, ma'am, we're getting on fine."

"You take good care of him for me, alright?" she asked.

"Yes, ma'am."

"You want them one at a time or should we catch them all?" Truman asked.

"Let's catch and hitch them up to the fence. They can use some gentling down."

By noontime, they about had the horses hooves worked over. The two boys were hard workers and they loosened up with him by the hour.

Truman finally got around to asking him, "We heard last night that you shot two of them bank robbers yesterday?"

"I did."

"What was that like?" Him and his brothers were all ears to hear his side of it.

"Not much to it. I sat in Mrs. Brown's shop all morning in a chair watching the bank's front door. They went inside I figured that they were going to rob the place. Mr. Phillps was on the roof. When the shooting started by an associate of their's in the street, he shot that man. I had a bead on the door when they busted out. The first guy out was going to shoot Phillips so I shot him. Then another robber came out blasting away. I shot him. The third was a lookout trying to get away. I shot his horse before he could get away. That stopped him."

"Whew, you were in the middle of it, weren't you?"

"It wasn't fun. I can tell you that. Rasping down these horse hooves was lots more fun."

They laughed.

"You know we heard about that robbery and your shooting last night." Truman said. "And me and Ferell were about afraid to come down here this morning and met you."

Rath laughed and clapped them on the shoulder. "I guess you know I'm one of you."

Truman looked around before he spoke, "We know that boy too that you roped for following you. He told us you was the meanest son of ah—man he ever met."

"He needed to believe that. That bunch of nightriders were cowardly mean. They shot one of my best horses for no reason."

Truman nodded. "There ain't no more talking about doing that again."

"Good. I can sleep with both eyes shut."

She was setting the table. "You boys looked so serious coming from the barn talking. Is something wrong?"

"Naw, we were talking about the high price of goats in Texas," Rath said.

They laughed and she frowned. "Men." And she was off to get the food to put on the table.

"We're going after that wagon tomorrow," Rath announced. "Truman says he can get away and go with us."

"I was thinking about letting you all go and me getting the dress fit before you change your mind."

"Fine, huh, guys?"

"You need me?" Ferrell asked.

"One of us better finish plowing," Truman reminded him. His brother agreed

So the deal was set.

The horses' hooves were all reshaped, their shaggy manes had been sheared and the dead winter hair curry combed out until they looked slick. They were going to use the big mare and the next largest one, a dark gelding for the team. Mary Ann assured him he'd find harness to fit them in her tac room. After doing her dishes, she and Ferell tried collars on them until they found ones that fit. Truman fit the harness to them.

The boys went home about five and shook Rath's hand before they left.

"We sure enjoyed the day," Truman said. "I guess you ain't half as bad as some would make you out to be. See you at sunup." Ferrel laughed at his brother's words and they left on their shanks mare.

He hugged her shoulder watching them hike off. "Nice guys. I guess they had worried about me being a bad guy this morning."

She turned him for the house, hugging his arm. "Why sure they have to be, you're marrying the outlaw queen."

Next morning, they hitched her buggy horse for her to go into town and get fit for her wedding dress. Then the two harnessed the team and led them off to go get the chuck wagon.

When they arrived at Darling's place, she came out in a wash worn dress with her sharp suspicious dark eyes glaring and nodded. "Them horse that you first brought are a long ways from being recovered. Glad you got some real ones."

He looked over the wagon. It didn't smell like a pig pen any longer and she had repaired the cupboard in back. She was handy as a pocket on a shirt.

"If I'd had the canvas I'd sewed you a new top *fur* it."

"You did good so far. When we get it fixed up with water barrels. We'll bring it back and you can start work making a top and a fly.'"

She nodded. "I want plenty of big needles, waxed thread and wax to seal the seams too. You can measure the canvas, but I want it so I can close it against the rain and me have a little privacy in a small corner."

"I can do that."

"By the way, how long is this business going to last?"

"A year and we'll see."

"Yeah. Well, that's long enough." She went out and helped them hitch the team. Busy fussing about the harness and everything, she told Truman. "These are a damn site better horses than them first plugs he brought me."

The boy never answered her. Obviously the cat had his tongue. Rath figured the farm boy'd never met the likes of Darling in his entire life—no doubt.

"I'll be back in a week with this wagon or Truman will. See you, Darling," He led Rebel that the youth had ridden over. The team acted a little snorty, but his man on the spring seat had taken charge of them. They jogged along going back under his command.

Half way home Rath had him stop. They took a break and chewed on some jerky.

"That is one tough woman back there," Truman said, shaking his head in disbelief.

"To be a camp cook you have to be."

"She'll sure be good then."

"Aw. She's got a big heart."

"I never saw it."

They laughed

At the ranch after dark, Mary Ann came out with a lamp. "You finally made it back. You need a lamp to get home?" she asked Truman.

"No, I'll run along alright. Thanks ma'am for offering me one."

"Well, wait, I can feed you."

"Maw will have some waiting when I get there. Thanks."

"Take my horse home," Rath offered to him.

"I'll be fine if you can unhitch'em?"

"Go on and thanks."

"See you in the morning."

"Sure," Rath said after him.

"Well, how was Darling?"

He kissed her. "Truman thinks she's the toughest woman he ever met."

"She alright?"

"Her? She's fine, but don't sound like she'll work over one week longer than a year for me. How was the dress fitting?"

"Alright, I hope you like it. Mrs. Brown said, she didn't blame me for marrying you."

"How was that?' He undid the single trees and then unhitched the neck yoke. He drove them over to the tac room, and un-harnessed them while she held the light. At last they started for the house with all the horses back in the pen.

"She said you were the coolest man she ever saw facing down those bank robbers. Said she was huddled down behind a wall hoping she didn't get shot."

"That was a good place for her. I'm glad they didn't shoot out her front window."

"Did you and Truman have fun today?"

"Yes, we did, but I'm glad I'm back here with you."

She kissed him.

Time flew and they took her buggy to the Saturday night social. She had him dressed in black wool pants, a starched white short, a new twead wool vest and a blue silk kerchief.

She wore his favorite blue dress and they took the buggy with the food in the box fit in the back she had cooked up for the purpose. They arrived in mid afternoon so she could help set up and also tell the crew about her pending wedding and what they needed to do for it.

He whittled on a cedar block, squatted on his haunches with some of the men folks in the yard. The sun was warm and he heard about new calves and a new horse bought to replace one that died of the colic the second day he used him plowing.

"Get a good replacement?" he asked.

"He's fair."

"I have two young horses that are mending. The man let them get pretty thin last winter. But they're three and should recover."

"You catch them loose draft horses been tearing up the wheat fields?" another husband asked.

"Yes."

"Glad you got them damn things. We've been chasing them for near a year."

Another man leaned over and said, "Hell, he shot three of them bank robbers too this week. Them wild horses weren.t nothing."

Before he could correct it to two, an older man said, "Ain't bad for a man we didn't even know a few weeks ago."

They laughed.

After dancing a lot, they drove home under the stars, kissy faced. The working crew of women she told him were excited about her wedding plans and planned to feed lots of folks that night.

"Just think after next week, we can take a bedroll and sleep on the ground."

He laughed. "I'd miss the buggy ride home with you."

"Shoot, we'll drive home then." She snuggled to him. "You know I'm not complaining, but he never liked to show any feelings like you do. You kiss me in front of folks and act like you're pleased."

"Every man has different ways. I loved your easy ways since you came and captured me at the first one. That Mrs. Cates, you know, almost kept me away that first night."

"Oh, I was collared with that and I don't like to lie?"

"Hey, no matter, it worked out well—" He reined up the horse and tried to see what was ahead in the brush beside the road in the starlight.

"What's wrong?" she whispered.

"I saw something like a horse moved in those bushes up there."

He filled his hand with his six gun. Keeping a sharp eye on every thing he could see in the dark, he nudged the horse to walk forward. Then a silhouette rode out and shot at them. The red orange flare of the muzzle came then the report.

"Hold him." He gave her the reins of the jittery horse and he jumped out, firing in the night at the would be retreating shooter. No way to hit them but they wouldn't know that. Two riders fled in the night and were gone.

"Who was it?" she asked.

"Cowards—more damn cowards."

"Are they gone?" she asked in a little girl's voice.

His breath raged through his throat. Who were those nightriders? He thought they were all in jail. He'd have to find these two and put them away.

"Are you alright?" she whispered.

His anger under control, he nodded, 'I'm fine. So that you and the horse are?"

"We're fine. Will they be back?"

"No, they shot too soon, they're gone. Cowards."

"Get in then and let's go home."

He slipped in beside her. "I'm sorry."

"No, I am mad for them ruining our fun evening."

He was too.

They drove on home, but the tension had ruined the perfect time. He sat up on the edge of the bed, still burning mad until she pulled him down with her, determined to settle his anger. She did.

Chapter 8

Morning, he sipped coffee in the sun lighted kitchen while she fixed oatmeal.

"Can we go to church today?" she asked.

"Sure."

"Good. You can meet my parents then."

"Will they shoot at me?"

"They never shot at him. But they sure didn't like him." She shook her head like she couldn't understand it—either.

He hitched the buggy horse and got ready to go. He wrapped the gun and holster in a piece of a blanket and stowed it under the seat. Then he went and put on his new clothes. In a short drive, they were speaking to the people at the Methodist Church and she introduced him to several. The usual morning reception she explained was in the back of the church with coffee and many sweets, breads and Danish set out.

"Rath." She touched his arm and took him along. She stopped in front of a nice looking middle aged couple. "I'd like you to meet my mother and father. John and Norma Temple."

He nodded to the gray haired man with his hat in hand and the straight backed woman who looked very somber. "Nice to meet you."

"Yes," her father said. But for Rath's part, the two showed little interest in either of them.

"I understand you caught those wild horses," he said.

"Yes, who owns them?"

He shook his head. "They've been running through crops and damaging property for over a year. I'm surprised someone didn't shoot them. No one could catch them before."

"They're dead broke. We fetched a chuck wagon with two of them on Friday."

"I wouldn't have believed that." He shook his head.

"Oh, he and Truman had no problems," Mary Ann said. "I want to invite you. Rath and I will be married next Saturday at the social."

"We don't attend that," her mother said cold as ice. "Come along, John."

"You have been invited," Mary Ann said. Her father nodded and her mother never acknowledged a thing.

Rath reached over and squeezed her hand. "You tried. You damn sure tried."

"Damn her anyway," Mary Ann said under her breath,

"You an only child?" Rath asked.

"Yes, do I act like one."

"No. But I can see she has her mind set. Sorry I asked you to do that."

"Not your fault."

He smiled. "No, I can't be blamed for their actions."

"Lets go find seats."

The hymns were song loud. The message was one of salvation and at the front door dutifully the pastor shook everyone's hands going out.

"You have a very fine young lady to marry, Mr. Macon."

"Yes, sir. I agree."

"May God bless your union. Have a good life together."

At the buggy, he removed his gun belt and put it back on. She waited on the seat and once he took the reins, she squeezed his arm. "She said, *we don't attend that*. I can't believe her."

"Hey, that's her loss. We'll lead our life and they can have theirs. Was everyone really afraid of those wild work horses?" He clucked to the horse and they went toward home.

"If they had owned some horses like yours, probably not. But chasing them on other draft animals might not work, so they chased them off into someone else's wheat."

He laughed. "I see what you mean."

The buggy rumbled over the wood plank bridge and up the next grade. He watched the clouds; they looked to be gathering. Warm enough it might rain.

Plans for his future business rumbled through his brain. In the interim of the next railhead move to Wichita, he wondered how it would affect his plans. No telling he'd proceed and let it flow.

"Are you worried?" she asked, with an elbow.

"I guess I was deep in thought about things I need to do."

"That's worried. As long as it is not about your future wife, I'll let you brood."

"Aw, I have lots riding on this cattle venture. I need it to work."

"I know you do. It will."

"I've got two good men to ramrod, and things should go smooth."

"You found them a few days ago, didn't you?"

"Yes, In Newton. I know both can manage men, they'll do their part. But what if it gets too big or no one will sell me their culls. That worries me."

"You will do it. Isn't that a shower out there?" She pointed out the shield of rain sweeping across the land in their direction.

"Yes. Get up horse, we're going to get wet." He slapped him with the lines. The rain was coming down hard and thunder crossed the sky when they reached the security of the barn's alleyway.

A little damp and still seated, he turned and kissed her. "We've made it."

The horse put up and the rest fed, they dashed for the house. Inside, he shed his boots and she made a face at him. "You don't have to do that."

"My house too. I love it."

"Good," she said and took his gun belt, buckled it and hung it on a wall peg. "Lunch comes next."

"Good, I'll watch you."

"I can work and be watched."

Thunder rattled the windows.

"You know that as much as I like rain. If I was out there herding cattle coming up here I'd be complaining."

He told her cattle drive stories and soon the kitchen smelled of her cooking. He thought he heard a horse and went to the back door. He could see in the rain Marshal Cone in a slicker, dismount and hitch his horse.

"We have company. The marshal is here."

"Is something wrong?" she asked.

"I don't know."

He opened the door and met the lawman. "Get in here. What brings you out on such a wet day?"

"I'm sorry to bother you two on Sunday." He handed Rath his hat and slipped out of his slicker. "But I got word that you might have more problems with night riders."

"Yes, they tried that last night. Someone almost ambushed us coming back from the social. They missed and rode off. You know who it is?"

"No. I got a note last night. Someone just must have had a guilty conscience about it happening. Sorry I am so late."

"That Springer boy mentioned someone named Snowberry the day I stopped him. Did he tell you he hired him to track me."

"Yes. But he's supposedly left the country. I went by where he once lived. The woman there said she didn't know where he went."

"What does he do for a living?'

Cone shook his head. "Probably steals for a living. He's not been caught is all I know."

"Then someone has hired him. He wouldn't have time from stealing to be a nightrider. Unless he was paid."

"I thought so, but I can't find any sign of him to answer my questions." Cone shook his head.

"Coffee?" Mary Ann asked holding the pot and they both nodded. She set out cups and filled them. "Food is next. You will eat with us?"

"Yes."

"Good."

When Cone headed back to town, the rain had quit. Nothing was settled, but while the warning came late, Rath knew there still was a movement to scare him out of the country. Nothing fit. Who had he pissed off?

He felt restless with the rain over for awhile. Better settle down and enjoy her company. To get in the swing of things, he dried dishes. The image of her aloft mother still struck him as strange. But even her father never offered to shake his hand. There was more there than he knew, but those two sure didn't want any part of their wedding. The two of them would live without it.

In the afternoon with her sitting on his lap on the couch and them smooching went well. He forgot about his concern over nightriders, aloft parents, and his new business all in one lump sum. Not complaining about one thing. That he was grateful for such a serene future bride—he'd had nothing, but tirades about everything from his past one.

"Tomorrow," he said. "I'm going down and locate a place to set up."

"Can I go along?"

"No. Much as I hate to tell you that. I don't know how long it will take. What it will involve and I promise to be back by Wednesday night."

"Good. I should have my new dress when you get back. Thanks for staying with me today. I needed you."

"Her ignoring you really upset you?"

"It shouldn't have, but it did."

"I saw that. But we can't let that take anything away from our life together."

"Yes, I agree, I had not spoken to her in years. I know now why I haven't."

He hugged her. "We won't miss them."

Chapter 9

He left for the Wichita Crossing before daylight on Red. He wrote out what he wanted Truman to do. Take the chuck wagon to town and have the blacksmith mount two water barrel holders on the sides. Pick up two new barrels to go in the holder and charge them at the store. Then bring the wagon back to her place. He could take Tuesday and Wednesday off to work at home and Thursday they'd work again.

"Can I use him to fix the garden fence?" she asked.

"Anything you need done is fine with me. If it dries out he can hoe too."

"Fine."

Then he went to saddle and rode out. It was cool after the rain and she wore a jacket accompanying him to the barn. He had on his jumper and vest figured that the temperature would rise up when the sun got up. He kissed her good bye and felt a little bit sad. He damn sure had a case on that woman. Short loping Red, he stopped a mile from the house, took the blanket out of the bedroll and wrapped in it. He'd certainly misjudged the sun warming up much at all. It was still spring in Kansas and she wasn't going to give him an inch. He'd had wife like that once.

He didn't dally long in Cherrydale. Went by and spoke to his banker about his plans, but missed seeing Cone and rode on. By late afternoon, he was in the Texas Saloon talking to the bartender named Harry, the one who backed his hand against the outlaw from Texas named Costrow

"How're things going for you up there?" Harry brought him a cup of coffee. The saloon crowd was thin and all huddled around the stove wearing scarves, and coats.

"Just fine. I need to rent a big place to sort lots of cattle and put up a crew or two."

Harry nodded. "There was some big outfit built a place they set up to winter some herds of their cattle here when they couldn't sell in '68. Big corrals and quarters."

"Who owns it?"

"Timothy Burns. He don't use it. Bet you could rent or buy it cheap. Ain't no one got any use for that much around here."

"I'll need to find him in the morning."

"That's easy. He has a farm about five miles east. Take the first wagon tracks east and watch for a two story white house on the left. He'll be around there."

"Thanks. Is there a warm place to sleep around here."

"We've got a back room, it ain't hot, but will beat being outside. Bring your roll in and sleep back there. You can stable your pony in the shed out back. There's some hay there too."

"I'm going to owe you a fortune."

Harry shook his head. "How's the railroad coming?"

"They're doing some grading I saw the work on the way down here today."

"That maybe be my pot of gold. They ever make this the cattle railhead, I should be able to sell this place and make a fortune."

"What will you do then?"

"Damned if I know. But I'm sure tired of the rift raft comes through here. Like that outlaw Costrow."

"He been back?"

"No, last I heard of him he got some work working for Colonel somebody. Anyway he ain't been in here in along time. But you must of made a good deal up there."

'I did and met a very nice lady, Mary Ann Cates. I'm getting married next Saturday night."

"Oh, I know that lucky lady."

"Mary Ann Cates?"

Harry whistled. "Charlie Cates widow? Ain't she the outlaw queen?"

"Yes." No need to tell him a thing. He'd meet her in the months ahead.

"Didn't I hear your name mentioned about some attempted bank robbers that got shot robbing the bank up there."

"That was me."

"Man, Costrow was lucky he didn't tangle with you. He'd be sprouting daisies."

"Bring me some stew."

The same teenage bar girl delivered it. She looked like she should be in school rather than working in the saloon, but she wasn't his worry. Like a puppet she made a nice smile for him delivering the bowl and spoon. "You need anything, mister, I'm available."

Outlaw Queen

"I'll be fine." Hell, he wasn't everyone's guardian. Her being there simply made him uneasy. Maybe she came from an orphanage, some of them sold young girls like her into bondage. He wasn't her keeper, but it was criminal. There was so little law in Kansas, but a few brave men like Cone. He watched her go back in the kitchen in the thread bare dress that made him feel cold.

After his meal, he rode out to the Timothy Burns' farm. He found the tall man cutting and busting fire wood with his boy of say of fourteen.

"Good day, sir," Burns doffed his cow-pie wool hat.

"Mr. Burns, I presume."

"Aye, they call me Tim."

"Rath Macon they call me Rath."

"This my son William."

He nodded to the boy. "I am interested in a round up camp you own."

"Aye, I should have expected that you being a drover and all. Get down from that fine horse and we'll have the wife make up some coffee. Lead the way."

"Marthie, we've got company. Rath Macon is here." He turned back to ask. "Where yeh from, Texas?"

"I was. I now live at Cherrydale."

"Oh, well, you made a good ride today."

"Good enough."

Marthie came putting on apron. She was hardly older looking than her step son. "Nice to meet'cha," she said.

"Yes, ma'am."

115

"Well, have a seat, sir," he offered pulling out a ladder back one around the large round table. "Are you in the cattle buying business?"

"Do you use cream, sir?" Marthie asked.

Rath shook his head to her and turned to him. "I going to try and buy some cattle. I've been driving herds up here and thought I'd get in the buying business."

"There is a section of land out there. Not much farming yet around it, so there won't be much complaining right now about loose cattle."

"I have not seen it, but if it suits me, could I rent it for one year with an option to buy it."

"Aye, I've no use for it."

"How much would you rent it for a year?"

"Two-fifty sound right?"

"If it was what I heard it is I can pay that."

Marthie brought the coffee and he could tell the way the man talked to her. She was not his original wife.

"Marthie and me been married a year, this June. Isn't she a lovely wife for such an ugly old men like me?"

"Yes, she is." His words made her blush as she poured coffee for them in china cups.

"Aye, William's mother died two years ago. Marthie lived down the road and I told the boy I would sure like to date her. He set it all up and in time, she agreed to come be my wife."

"Don't listen to him, sir. He's a sweet generous, patient man with the likes of me. Will you eat some of my Danish?"

"I'd love some."

His son leaned over. "That's the best part of her being my mom—her cooking."

"Well. I'm certain Rath doesn't need any more history about us. I would price the place at six thousand dollars with a one year option."

"I'll have to see it first. The price sounds fair enough."

"I'll warn you some of it is not plow land."

"Let's say we have a deal. Do you get mail at the Crossing?"

"Yes, why?"

"Well, I will mail you a letter sealing the deal if it suits me, because I need to go back home and get married myself this Saturday.

"And who is the lucky lady?"

"Mary Ann Cates."

"Isn't she the—"

"Yes, she's Charlie Cates's widow. I don't care for it, but many people have christened her the outlaw queen."

"Well, the best of luck to you and her, sir."

"Did she ever ride with them?" his son asked.

"No. She thought he was cattle buyer for a firm in Ft. Scott. Knew nothing at all about his other life and received a letter from a gang member when he was killed was all her contact was with them."

Burns nodded like he was in deep thought. "Then I will check my mail for your reply."

"You understand I will be back here in two weeks to take possession of the place if all works. You can check with my banker in Cherrydale if you need any more about me or the operation."

"I don't think that would be necessary, Rath. You're a very open person. My dealings with Texans have all been above the board. I hated those men did not continue to rent it. But I understand their business folded up."

"I'll try not to do that." He made her blush thanking her for the pastry.

The two males walked him to his horse and saw him off. The weather had warmed and clouds were rolling in. He decided to see the place he'd rented and rode the distance to arrive before the sun went down.

The setup had a main house not very big with a stove. Then a few smaller apartments and a larger bunk house. Two outhouses, sheds and some tall pole corral to hold lots of cattle. They'd taken the squeeze chute with them. Plus more sheds and pens for horses with some old hay still around. A very extensive set up that suited him. The price was right, but as a farm which most folks coming in the country wanted, it was not that.

He rode back to the Crossing in the dark and after another bowl of stew, he slept in Harry's barn feeling satisfied he was lucky to rent the Burns place. And he thanked his bartender friend as well. One more night's sleep and he'd be headed back to his to be bride. He really missed her warm sweet body sleeping with him. Giving a shudder, he pulled the blanket up and slept.

In the predawn, he saddled Red and went to find some breakfast. He found Harry and his young bar maid in the kitchen. The two were busy making biscuits, gravy and frying eggs.

"Don't you ever sleep Harry?" Rath asked from the back door.

"Not much, we ain't had much business this winter. Me and Cozy here been the only two and we've had to do it all. Course it's better than nothing, ain't it Cozy?"

"Yeah, we eat anyway."

"Where did Cozy come from?" Rath asked about the girl who called herself Claire, taking a seat at the table as directed by Harry.

"Cozy came last fall. Her step father was using her. You know what I mean?"

Rath nodded.

"They were passing through. He came looking for her but I hid her here. Guess it was what I thought I should do. They went on without her."

"I see. If I give you some money will you buy her some clothes?"

"I guess." Harry shrugged. "Guess I hadn't thought about it. She could use some couldn't she?" He turned to the girl. "Would you wear some clothes if he bought you some?"

"Certainly."

"I'll do that," Rath said and put two dollars on the table.

She brought him a plate full of dutch oven biscuits piled high with white gravy. At the sight of it, he shook his head. "I can't eat all that."

"I bet you do, mister. And thanks."

He did and rode back to Cherrydale, told McDonald about the place he'd rented. Spoke to Cone over at the lunch counter about things. The lawman had no answers to his questions about the nightriders and after a meal that Marle insisted he eat, he rode for Mary Ann's place. It was twilight when he dismounted at the barn to unsaddle.

Dogs barking him home, she came out on the run refreshed looking in a button up the front house dress that fit her willowy form. They hugged and kissed.

Then he unsaddled, answering as many questions as he could for her about the Crossing operation and what he had rented. He finished with, "It looks a little cowboy rough, but it will work fine for my needs."

"So when do the cattle come up from Texas?"

He swept her up in his arms and kissed her before she could protest. "After our honeymoon."

"Oh, after that."

"Yes, after that."

She shook her head as if in dread. "I can sure tell when you come home and carry me inside what you want."

"Oh?"

She drew a large inhale up her slender nose. "And I want the same things too."

They both laughed and kissed. If God ever fulfilled a cow puncher's dream, he sure did with her.

The next day boys did some planting for her in the garden. He made some plans on paper at the kitchen table. The clock was ticking. Frank Wade could be headed for the Crossing with those horses. Other things on his mind were the chuck wagon and Darling— he needed his cook set up at his gathering ranch.

Chapter 10

They woke up friendly in the predawn and had another session of fierce lovemaking before they dressed and went into the kitchen. Out of the east kitchen window he saw a strange horse switching his tail at the barn. Deliberately, he strapped on his six gun.

"What is it?" she asked.

He waved his hand for her to stay inside. "I'll go see."

A concerned frown crossed her face. "Be careful."

The man he found at the barn hadn't shaved in a few days. He stood back inside the open doors and nodded politely. "Sorry to bother you, mister."

"Can I help you?"

The man swallowed and nodded. "Is this the Charlie Cates' place?"

"Yes, but he's been dead for quite a while."

" I-I knew that, but I needed a place to rest a few hours. I won't bother you or her. I just need a few hours and I'll be gone."

He wondered why her dogs had not barked. "What did you do to her dogs?"

"Oh, I'm good with dogs." He beamed. "I know all about them. Less they're dead mean, I can get them hushed in a few minutes."

"I guess you're on the run?"

"Yeah, I am, but no danger to you or her like I said before."

"You know these people have shunned her because she was Charlie's widow. Your coming here won't help that one bit."

"I knew Charlie well, mister. He was like a brother to me. He told me how pretty she was. I've never seed her. He told me how good she was. I thought she must be Jesus' Mary. And all I want is five-six hours rest."

Rath looked at the ground. Time to make up his mind. "Get that horse out of sight, grain him and be gone by dark. You got food?"

"Yes. I don't know your name mister, but God bless you. I mean God bless you."

"I'm taking her away for the day. You be gone by sundown."

"My name is Finest Yates. And I won't tell a soul about this I swear."

"Just be gone by sundown."

"Oh, I will." He went and pulled his horse inside the alley way. "No one will know I'm here or been here."

"Thanks."

He left for the house. Right or wrong, he'd done it. Given comfort and aid, no doubt to a killer and a wanted man.

Out of breath, she opened the back door for him. "Did he leave? Who is he?"

He herded her inside. "His name is Finist Yates. He rode with Charlie. He's a desperate wanted man who needs a day of rest."

"And you told him what?"

"He could rest here today but he had to ride away before sundown."

"Will he do that?"

"Yes, he simply needs to rest."

She ran to put his food on the table and nervously poured him coffee. "I-I never gave them any aid or comfort."

He hugged her. "Easy, I believe you. This man is on the verge of going crazy. He is desperate and polite. He will be gone by nightfall. I did this, not you. Eat your breakfast, we'll go get your wedding dress."

She dropped on the chair and held her head. "I never—"

He clapped her forearm on the table to get her attention. "I don't doubt one word. I felt sorry for him. He maybe the worst killer in the world. But in this case, he's human and in need. Six to ten hours won't hurt our reputation or yours."

In surrender, she agreed.

"Now eat, you're going to need your strength."

She smiled at him through wet lashes. "You are such a tough man."

"Tough? I felt mushy telling him he could rest here."

"No. Other men would have panicked. You did the right thing for another human."

"Let's eat and I'll hitch up the buggy and we'll go get that dress."

She stood up and hugged his face to her bosom. "Oh, Rath. I am so glad we have each other."

"So am I. Now eat."

She obeyed him and he finished his food and went to harness the buggy horse. He never looked for Yates. He set the rig up ready to go and drove down to the house. She came out under a scarf for the wind and they left for Cherrydale.

She looked back anxiously, then turned and settled down beside him as the horse made the turn on the county road. "What else will we do today, besides get the dress?"

"Oh. Who knows? Wade in some creek maybe or see some new land."

She hugged his arm. "I like both ideas. I only dreamed I'd ever have a man who'd do those things with me."

Regardless of acting like he'd forgotten Yates, the man would be on his mind all day. So it didn't interfere with her having fun, he'd be sure that it didn't happen again.

In town, he parked in front of the Mrs. Brown's shop and helped her down. Once on the boardwalk, a woman named Mrs. Parks stopped her and they visited about the coming up wedding.

Some how their wedding plans had made her much more palatable to these women. Like she was going to join society over her marriage to him. Damn, he excused himself and went over to the general store. He talked to Vance McGregor about his account and the barrels he'd charged.

"Oh, no worry. McDonald at the bank said he's backing you. Anything you need let me know."

"I will need a coil of hemp rope to make lariats out of."

"That I will have to order, but it should be here in two weeks."

'That will work. Next week, I'll need a barrel of flour, a barrel of corn meal, couple sacks of brown beans, several slaps of bacon and I'll leave the rest to my camp cook, Darling."

"Do I know her?"

"I doubt it. She's a character and lives up toward Newton, but I think she can feed and nurse maid the hands I hire."

"I won't forget the name that's for sure." He chuckled about it.

"You won't forget her either. You have a shower head for a sheepherder's shower."

McGregor shook his head.

"Fine, I can get a one made up at blacksmith shop here. I want it for the place down at the Crossing."

"Is there a wind mill?"

"No, but I figure I'll need one."

The store man nodded. "I know of some mills that are for sale."

"I'd take one if it's a bargain?"

"Can you haul it?"

Rath shrugged. "If I have to."

"I'll find one as close to there as possible. That's west of the Crossing, huh?"

Rath agreed and he could see her across the street at the door of the shop searching for him. He excused himself and went to join her.

She gave him the new dress all wrapped in tissue like paper. He strapped it on the box in back then joined her.

"How are you doing?" she asked when he joined her on the seat.

"I guess I need my cook and the wagon down at the Crossing."

"How will you do that?"

"Get her moved down there."

She laughed. "Your darling?"

"Yes," He smiled at her teasing. "And I may need that done before our big night."

"The wagon is here?" she asked.

"Yes, the water barrels mounted and the supplies can be loaded in it. She was going to replace the top, but she can do that down there and those cowboys that Wade hired can help her."

"I can go get her for you."

"No, she probably has a wagon load to take with her."

"Could the boys go get and move her?"

"That might be the answer."

Saturday, they spent alone at her place. The business could wait. In fact the whole world could wait. He polished his boots. She flittered around about this and that like what ribbon to wear in her hair. They ate lunch in silence like a wall had come between them. But when they finished and each rose silently to their feet. Then without a word, he swept her up in his arms. She kissed him and then whispered in his ear. "I had the same idea, but thought it was too brazen."

"Never brazen. It's our world, not anyone else's and I can't stand another minute apart from you any longer."

In the bedroom they became lost in each others arms and needs for a long while.

The school house gleamed on the rise in the bright April sun, when he drove the horse and buggy up the hill. Several of her friends and neighbors were already there. The women folks oohed and awed about her dress and they led her off. He joined the men and they went over to sit on benches under some early leafing out trees swaying in the wind. He'd not noticed the wind being that strong, but there were many other things he'd missed as well on the drive.

In no time, they had him lined up at the podium and the preacher from her church, Reverent Imes was waiting with the good book open. A fiddler played some soft waltz music and she came up the aisle.

"This day we come to this place to join these two people as man and wife. . . ." The rest was far away and he was never certain if he said everything right on his part. But when Imes announced he could kiss the bride—he did. *Thank you, God.*

Where did the gold ring come from? He'd never thought about one. The other ring had cost him two hundred dollars. She probably threw it away gong to San Antonio in a huff. Forget her, he had the loveliest wife in Kansas.

There was a big crowd there for the event and the schoolhouse was packed full of folks. They were surrounded by well-wishers and he recalled the night she introduced him to so many and then they were left alone. Him and the outlaw queen—this night they acted like they were all sisters to her and would not quit.

They were offered the head of the food line and he wasn't certain he was going to be able to eat. However she kept him in place, he ended the food tables with his plate covered with too much food. They retired to a wall bench to discover there were presents to be opened as well.

Well after midnight they arrived back at their place. Unhitched the horse. Put him up and staggered to the house. They undressed going though the house and fell into each others arms on the bed and kindled fire enough in their brains and muscles to complete their marriage.

The next five days were a whirl wind of events. They took picnics and roamed the land. He drove her down to the buying headquarters and they examined the new place. She met Ward and the three new cowboys—Harry had sent them out there. Wiggins, Shorty and Beaver were their names.

She laughed about the hands, who acted excited to meet her and Ward impressed her. He'd had those three shaping the bare foot horses feet with rasps that he got at the store. The horses sounded like they were sound enough and Shorty told him about a half dozen were still kinda buggery.

She made them all pancakes the next morning and they bragged on her. He promised them a cook soon and they went home. It rained a little before they reached her place, but nothing could dampen the honeymooners.

He rode over leading Red and got Ferrel to take the wagon up to get Darling. He told him to take a bedroll because by the time he got her and moved her, it would take at least two days. Harry in the Texas Saloon would tell him how to get out to the headquarters. With a list of supplies for him to get in Cherrydale, Ferrel said he'd get it done. He started for town driving the wagon and left the two of them at the house.

"I want to go with you next week," she said.

"Let me have a few days to straighten up things down there."

She agreed.

Chapter 11

He sent Ferrel with the chuck wagon to go by the store to get the supplies and then go get Darling and take her to the Crossing. He felt they certain they would not reach the cow camp until Thursday evening. On the list of supplies to get, he had her order for canvas, needles, bee wax and waxed thread. Also a map from the Crossing to the camp and he promised the teenager he'd be there later in the week.

"Me too," his wife promised, then she said,, "Truman is looking after things here."

"You better get packed then," he teased her.

"What will we do with all that time?" she asked when Ferrel was gone to hitch up.

"Oh, fish and fiddle." He put on his hat to go join the boy and get him gone,

They camped and the weather cooperated. Fished in some small rivers on the way, and even a small lake. She fried some pan fish crisp and they ate them shedding bones and laughing. The two bigger ones caught were catfish they hauled out on their willow poles. She rolled them in corn meal and they ate fish until they thought they'd bust.

They waded small streams and swam naked in a few deeper holes he found. Then on Wednesday he got serious about getting over there and drove to the cow camp. Things were busy and his bride drew lots of looks from the crew members in their passing by them. In a clean apron, her dark hair in a severe bun, Darling came to the shade of the chuck wagon with the new canvas top. She must have worked the whole crew on her project to have it completed in such a short time.

"Darling, this is my wife Mary Ann."

"Glad to meet'cha, ma'am."

"Nice to meet you too," Mary Ann said in return

"Well, does it look good enough?" She waved at the new top.

"Looks like it was done with great care." He stood back to look at it. "I see this end closes well for your privacy. Are you getting along?"

"Both ends close. Feeding working boys ain't no problem. They'll eat you out of house and home. Make lots of it and fill a sweet tooth and you have it made."

"I thought you could do it. Good. Come on," he said to his bride. "I need to talk to my foremen."

"Looks to me like they've done lots of work on the setup."

"They're moving along," he said, pleased with the progress showing. Gates were repaired on the pens, broken window glass replaced in the main building. There were some older sidewall tents set up. Maybe they were for the hands—they'd been used and had taken on the brown color of old canvas.

Ira came with a quirt hanging around his wrist to meet him. He shed his felt hat and smiled at her. "Howdy ma'am."

"This is Mary Ann, my new bride Ira."

"Hey, Boss man, you got the pick of the litter up here."

"Thanks, how's it going?"

"We'll be ready in a few days. One of the boys said they knew where there was a squeeze chute you could buy."

"Where is he?"

'I'll locate him and send him to see you. I see you have a tent on that pack horse."

"Yes, set it up. I should have a windmill coming in a week or so. Hand pumping water isn't much fun."

"We been taking them the horses to the river twice a day. Where do you want that tent set up?"

"On that rise up there." He turned to her. "You want up there?"

"Fine."

"What else?"

"When we begin to buy cattle we'll need to increase the payroll. But till then we'll kind make do."

Ira agreed. "Better talk to Frank about it, but the mustang man he bought the horses from wants to sell you some more. They're good cowponies like the ones we have now."

"I savvy that. Give me that lead on your two pack horses. Ma'am if you show me where up there you want this tent stood up. Me and some boys will tend to it."

"Go ahead, Mary Ann, I'll go find Frank and when you get things like you want–" He checked the sun time. "Darling should have lunch ready by then. I'll meet you up there."

They parted and he found Frank working on a saddle in one of the sheds. Small nails in his mouth he nodded and went to applying them to the saddle with a short handled farrier's hammer. He removed the ones he didn't use and cleared his throat. "I bought some extra saddles cheap. They ain't worth much but they'd beat riding bare back if you ain't got one."

"That's a good idea." They shook hands.

"We're getting it in shape. Things look alright to you?"

"Yes, we're making progress. I spoke to Ira. He said the horse seller needs to sell some more."

Frank nodded "To be honest he bought too damn many."

"I'd like to hold off spending a lot of money 'till we see how the cull buying goes."

"We will need some more. If I tell him we'll take sixty more when things get under way, I can pick the real good ones now."

"I don't see anything wrong with that. Hey, in three weeks to a month we probably will need more horses. What else?"

"One of the boys knows about a squeeze chute and we can put it right where their's was."

"How much?"

"Ten bucks."

"Go get it."

"I thought you'd say that. Someone stuck their head in here a minute ago and said you'd brought your bride."

"Yes, she's here."

The chuck wagon triangle began ringing.

"Well, "Ira said. "I had my doubts about a woman cook but you were right. She beat a hundred grubby men called themselves cooks. She ain't no society lady and you get crabby around her she'll haul off and smack you with a big spoon, but the food is damn good."

Frank got up and reset his hat. "I damn sure hope this works. I like the whole operation you planned."

"I do too. I have lots riding on it working."

"When are you going to try to buy some?"

"I figure go scout the first ones coming north next week."

"I'd sure sold the ones I had along with my herd when I got this far north."

"Some folks won't. They'll be convinced they can sell them like they have a auction fro anything up here."

Frank nodded gravely. "And those buyers will cut back several head and you'll feel like a damn fool."

"We will soon see. Oh, I have a windmill coming to set up. What do we need to do?"

"I got a couple of boys know all about them. We'll do some planning to be ready. We can sure use a tank too."

Rath agreed. "That can be arranged. A black smith's making a shower head."

"We'll need some tubs we can put on a platform and hook the shower under them. Heat it a little in the day before you use it won't hurt. This well water must come from the Artic."

Both he and Frank headed for the fly where the hands were gathered around his wife in line. Darling had the canvas top to her rig tied down and the strong south wind barely rumbled it. She knew the force of Kansas breezes.

He shook hands with all the men there and noted their names, Bob, Curley, Jess, and so on. They were all wiry enough looking and this wasn't their first trip.

Golden brown chicken fried steak, mashed potatoes, thick flour gravy and biscuits. Those cowboys bragged on her as they filled their tin plates.

"Raisin-apple cobbler is in the last Dutch oven. If you drop my big spoon in the dirt you'll have to do the dishes today," she announced and they all laughed.

"Helluva great cook." Short Bob elbowed him. "I ain't ate like this in my life on a job."

"He ain't lying either boss man," the man behind him said, then dropped his voice. "You ever met her sister, the one run off with her husband."

Rath shook his head.

"She must be one helluva cook for him to ever leave Darling."

Rath chuckled and Mary Ann turned to look up at him.

"I'll tell you later."

She nodded and went ahead finishing off filling her plate. "These guys may get too fat to ride."

"They damn sure might."

Her evening meal were brown beans with onions, meat and just enough spices to make them sharp tasting. Her corn bread in his mouth was like cake and Rath noticed the hands did her dishes and pans for her after this meal.

"Were you ever in the café business?" he asked Darling when she came over at the end to eat her plate of beans standing up.

"Nope."

"Well, your food's great. We need to find you a swamper."

"I can make it feeding this few hands. But I was going to ask you for one when the rosters filled out."

"Them boys damn sure appreciate you I can see, them doing the dishes at night."

She nodded and took another spoon full of beans. "They're real men. Tough and soft hearted as well. Ain't no big chore when they treat you so nice."

"Why don't you sit down with us," Mary Ann said.

"Thank you, ma'am. I appreciate the invite."

"Hey, you don't need an invite with us," Mary Ann said,

She scooted in and set down her plate on the plank table. "You mind if I ask you something?"

"I guess not."

"Last couple of years, I've been hearing all about an outlaw queen."

Mary Ann smiled. "Well, you've met her now."

Darling laughed. "I ain't making fun of you, but you don't look like no outlaw queen to me."

"That's fine," Mary Ann said blushing. "I never knew what I was supposed to look like either."

'Well, you're sure the prettiest one I ever met anyway."

He listened to some frogs croaking. Darling was right, she was the prettiest outlaw queen in the west. Things were taking shape in his camp, he felt more settled, but meeting the herd drovers came next.

Chapter 12

After the third day, he took her home. He needed to ride down in the Indian Territory and meet the first ones headed for Newton, which was a bedroll packing trip and too much exposure for her. He asked for a week to ten days and he'd be back, she agreed. But it was hard parting the next morning before daybreak. He kept closing his eyes rocking her in his arms at the back door.

He finally set out on Red for the cow camp. He missed lunch, but Darling, fed him any way. She kept saying, "You've got the prettiest and smartest girl I know."

With a grin, he agreed, already feeling bad that he had to leave her.

"They went after the squeeze chute," Ira said joining him.

"Good. We should hear about the windmill soon."

"That would be alright. You heading south."

"Yeah, I need to test my plan."

"Ah hell, it'll work."

"We'll see."

He rode over south into the Indian Territory the next morning and by dark he had not encountered a single herd. Making camp, he wondered if he had lost track of dates. It was April and there should be some brave ones coming up the trail. Day two, he found the Dawson Brothers. A couple of bearded men who looked more like preachers rather than drovers. They had a pack train for grub. Trail folks called those kind, *a greasy sack outfit.* No chuck wagon and the crew looked like they'd been drug through a knot hole to him. Their horses were slab sided.

He palavered with them for about an hour. But despite the fact they'd never been up there before, they scoffed at his notion there was no market in Newton, Kansas for culls and cows.

Alfred, the talker of the two, told him they'd been trading cattle since they were boys. "We ain't never missed making money in any deal in our lives."

"Men, you are going to find that you are in on the biggest market for big frame steers, the rest is worth nothing. They buy only big frame steers the rest sell for two dollars a head and they feed the carcasses to hogs."

He thanked them. They offered to feed him. But no one around there looked like they'd washed their hands since leaving Texas. He excused himself rather than risk it. Mounted on Red, he said, "If you need to sell the culls, bring them back down to the crossing. I can use some of them."

"Thanks to you too, mister," Alfred said.

He ate some jerky for supper. *Greasy Sack outfit* stuck in his mind as he sat on his bedroll, gnawing on the jerky. Guys like them gave the Texas cattle drovers a bad reputation. Those poor cowboys never had a decent meal all the way north. He'd bet good money some had even died of food poisoning. Not enough horses to have one to ride for every five-six days so they maintained their weight on the graze. He shook his head; his first stop had been disappointing. But these men did not represent the rest of the ones coming north. He slept unsettled and headed out early.

The Bar T W looked like sharp outfit on the move. He could see large two-three year old steers almost trotting headed north in the mid morning sunshine. Swing rider pacing them. That mean to pick up the speed, they rode in closer to the leaders. To slow them they moved more aside. The bell steer, a large blue one, kept them in line and behind him. No one challenged his leadership or he shook his own horns enough to impress the underlings who tried to pass him.

A rider on the scout came loping up. "Can I help you sir?"

"Where is the boss?"

"Follow me." He whirled his buckskin horse to head south and they keep to the high ground. They met two men, one in a business suit on a high point.

The man in the suit was John Harmon, his second in charge was Tub Reagan when they shook hands.

"What can we do for you?" Harmon turned to the rider. "Thanks Neal."

The rider rode off on his scout.

"I doubt I can do much for you, sir. I'm buying limpers and culls at the Wichita Crossing that buyers won't accept."

Harmon nodded. "Let's keep moving. I have some. What do you pay?"

"Eight dollars a head. We know they won't be worth anything at Newton. That isn't much but it beats getting nothing or two dollars for them."

"A smart business. How many limpers do we have, Tub?"

"Maybe two dozen?"

Harmon nodded. "The boys riding drag might hug your neck. We'll cut them out." They rode at a jog. "How far ahead is that worthless Dawson Brothers outfit. I'm concerned with getting our herds mixed with their's."

"Maybe five miles."

"I thought so. Tub go have Neal find us a route around them. We'd be weeks separating them out."

"We can do that," Tub said and left in a high lope to catch his man.

Harmon turned back to Rath. "You're the one lost the TH—Ranch?"

"Yes."

"And you're already set up here?"

"I have a solid banker backing me. It was a long ride up here from Texas. You know that culls have brought two bucks up here. I think we can recondition or sort off the smaller ones and make a little money."

"Shame I didn't get a chance to invest."

"I needed someone now. My man is solid. I have a headquarters already."

Harmon laughed. "You buying out the Dawson's?"

"He said he ain't never lost on a cattle deal in his life and he'd sell them in Newton."

"That ragtag outfit won't sell their junk to anyone. We need a trail organization on this road. People like him barred from it. We'll have them cut out when we cross. I hope you get rich as hell at this."

"So do I."

"Oh, your ex wife is going to marry the Hill heir."

"Good luck to him."

Harmon chuckled. "I knew that would make you envious."

His first promised cattle. He shook the man's hand. "I hope he has lots of money, she spent all of mine."

By nightfall, he had spoken to two more trail drivers. One was a maybe and another thought he had fifty head.

The next morning having breakfast with Ed Thompson of the BBK outfit, he ate his pancakes and coffee, thinking what Darling must be serving his crew. They'd soon be busy. But her food was more tasty then these flat flap jacks and watery syrup.

He felt the first hundred head was a good start. He thanked Thompson for his putting him up and rode for the crossing, staying wide of the herds to not spook them. At sundown he and Red splashed the crossing. He ate supper with Harry and Claire at the Texas Saloon. She looked much better in her new clothing.

Before breakfast, he rode in his own cow camp. Darling stepped out to greet him.

"Do some good?" she asked.

"Yes," he said.

"Well, then I've got a job." She laughed and wiped her hands on the clean apron. "I better get busy."

"You have a job, Darling."

With a cup in his hand, Ira stepped out from under the fly as he hitched Red. "You must have done good."

"I think in the week ahead we'll have our first hundred head and be started."

"I thought you'd make it work. You going home today?"

"I may need a fresh horse and leave Red here."

"I wondered. The Injun that Frank has herding the horses, can get you one. We'll put Red up in the pens and feed him."

"Good enough."

"How high was the river?"

"I never noticed." Rath frowned at him. What did he mean?

"It's rising each day. I figure from snow melt or rain out west. We've been marking it each morning and evening when we take the horses down there."

"Good idea. We might warn our drovers coming north that there is rise coming."

"What do you want me to do?" Ira asked cupping his coffee in his hands.

"I'll make you a list and you send your best man to tell them."

Ira agreed.

"Get me that fresh horse, I want to go home for a few days."

"No problem. She's about got breakfast ready. I ain't figured why her man ran off, ain't a rider in this camp wouldn't marry her."

"You don't know her sister." Rath laughed.

"You ever met her?"

Rath shook his head and sent him off with a grin.

After eating her fluffy pancakes, syrup, peaches and coffee, he sat back and studied his crew busy eating. If he did one thing right—it was hiring the insistent Darling. He asked her if she needed anything before he left.

With a smug head shake, she smiled at him. "I am just enjoying this job to death."

"Good, keep enjoying it. I'm going to see my wife."

"You kiss her for me. She's neat."

"I will."

He rode thru Cherryvale and spoke to McDonald. They had a good conversation and agreed their plan was going to work. McDonald told him that McGregor at the mercantile had a windmill ready to roll for his cow camp.

"I'll get to him. We'll sure need it."

"Tell the Mrs. hello," McDonald said, rose and shook his hand. "You need anything let me know. This is going to work."

He stopped by the grocery and talked to the store keeper. Plans were made to arrange for hauling it. Coming out, he talked briefly with Marshal Cone on the boardwalk.

"You learn any more about night riders?"

Cone shook his head. "You must have put the fear of God in them."

"Good, so they don't bother her."

Cone agreed. "I miss you. Not many folks I can talk to about things. How's the business going?"

"We're started."

"Good. I bet it works."

"It has to. Need me she'll know where I am."

He short loped the grey horse. A stout mustang, shorter than Red, but he was tough as a pine knot and smooth riding. It was late afternoon when he came up the lane to her house. The dogs met him with enthusiasm.

She burst out on the back porch. The excitement in her eyes made him feel warm all over. He swung down, dropped the reins and ran to swing her around.

Gray in the corral, they rushed to the house and he toed off his boots in the back hall. Talking at a hundred miles a minute, they finally grew quiet, face to face. He closed his eyes and kissed her deep in reverence to their heaven sent union.

"Damn I missed you," he said, looking deep into her eyes.

"No more than I have."

Chapter 13

The McEntosh boys had everything working at Mary Ann's place. Even her windmill spun quieter. The garden plants were making efforts to emerge. He walked around the home place in the first light. Freshness of the morning had a scent of the new grass and trees beginning to emerge in new green hue on the branches. He loved the hill country of Texas but the rolling Kansas blue stem country felt equally inviting and had none of the after taste of his previous home.

The two dogs bouncing around hoping he had some work for them—it was a neat time to just inhale it all. Some time a man felt he had to thank God and savor his blessings, this morning he was doing all that studying the soft wheat blades shifting in the growing wind.

She came out on the porch and shouted, "Your breakfast is ready."

He waved, the dogs barked over his, "Coming."

So far his cattle operation looked alright. But this was only the first days of the summer season. There must be two hundred thousand head coming north bawling their way up the trail in long lines, driven mostly by boys on the adventure of their life. And standing near the head of that great trail, he felt like the overseer for what would come. Before he put his boot on the bottom step, he could recall his first trip up there. The nights and days that his belly cramped over events and decisions he had to make. Solemn burials of boys who died in river crossings, stampedes, horse wrecks, snake bite and pneumonia. How later he'd have to tell their mom how sorry he was about her loss and how great they'd been. But the markers would be stomped down by the time they rode back home that summer and their dear mothers would never decorate their graves with flowers or for that matter know exactly where they were located.

"You look sad," she said and kissed him when he came inside.

"No reason," he said, hugging her around the waist and swinging her back and forth. "I have you. A great breakfast and we'll have a good day like always."

"You better eat it, or it'll be cold. You and the dogs have a good search?"

He toed off his boots. "We sure did."

"They're good company. They make me feel safe out here."

He kissed her forehead, then washed up at the sink.

"Several men have stopped by wanting to buy some of your work horses. I told them you'd be back by the end of the week."

"I could have priced them to you and you could have sold them."

She shook her head. "Trading horses isn't my job. You handle that."

They sat down at the table, he said a short grace and she passed him the platter of eggs and bacon. Next with care he buttered some hot biscuits and then used her blackberry jelly to top the butter. Living like a king.

he decided and turned to her. "You have any big requests you'd like filled."

"No."

"Damn woman, you're easy to please."

"No, I've spent the last two years—alone here. But I've made my own way, still I kept looking out the living room window hoping that someday a man would come for me—a good man. And he did. . . ."

"Hey, don't cry."

"I'm sorry. . . ."

He dapped at the tears on her cheek with a napkin.

"Oh, Rath, I can't believe he was saving me for you. But I am so grateful it was worth the wait."

"The good Lord works in mysterious ways."

"There are times I thought, well, I'll just have to grow to be an old spinster as the outlaw queen right here."

"Pretty as you are? No way, why I was lucky to find you."

In a rush, he grabbed his coffee cup, took a quick gulp, and scooped her up in his arms. She blinked her wet lashes in surprise and he was headed with her to the bedroom. At her realization of his intent, her free laughter filled the room. With care, he side stepped with his load through the doorway and used his sock foot to close it behind them. Didn't take much to tip his hand with her about his intentions.

That afternoon they drove to town, he talked to McDonald about more arrangements. He planned to let them cash their cattle receipt at the bank for the time being. Wichita Crossing was too wide open to operate a bank office down there. Both of them felt better than using a locked strong box to hold the money and worry about all the drifters who'd drooled over the contents.

Cone told him he had a lead on Snowberry and another man he had no name for, but they were both probably in Missouri. Rath thanked him and when Cone asked, he said, "The cripple buying looks alright."

Sunday after church and dinner, he went back to the cow camp. Hard to leave his wife, but he promised she could stay for a week down there later—and soon. He also told her the price for the once thin young team was two hundred. They looked real good, shinny coats and filling out. He felt they would make some money on his investment. Beside they looked like a good matched team. Farmers liked matches—a big horse and a little horse team kinda looked like you were out on bad economic ground.

She nodded that she heard him then kissed him good bye.

He arrived down there after supper. Darling came out from her wagon in the last light of sundown and welcomed him back.

"You hungry, boss man?"

"I could eat."

"Climb down. I have some grub."

"Thanks." Hitched his horse and took a place at the table under her shade. The night wind was still up and clapped the canvas roof in the last light of sundown. She returned with a coal oil lamp and hung it above him on a hook and slid a plate heaped with meat and potatoes before him.

"How's the wife?" She slid in across from him.

"Good. How's the crew?"

"Oh, they're concerned about the river. It's still rising. Getting deeper."

"That must be a big snow melt in Colorado," he said, breaking open a biscuit.

Ira arrived and took a seat beside Darling. "There were two drovers here while you were gone. They're south a ways and want to talk about selling some culls." He handed Rath a piece of paper with names on it.

"They came to the right place, didn't they?' Rath smiled at him pleased. "Darling said the river is still rising."

"Hell, I came up here three years ago with a herd and waited two weeks to get across that damn Arkansas. It was a mile and a half wide forever:

"I was late that year getting started," Rath said. He never regretted that though it was not planned. He couldn't get all the ends together to get away and it turned out to be fortunate for him. The biggest problem about flooding rivers was that backed up large herds got mixed and they got impossible to sort, One of the worst situations that could happen and it did at road blocks like prairie fires, tornados and bad storms as well to have all your cattle blended with another herd.

Frank came over and talked with them under the slightly swinging lamp.

"Going to blow in another storm," Franks said, tossing his head at the wind.

Rath agreed. "But Kansas is like this every spring."

"I'd like for one year for them to have a mild one."

"No way. Did you send word to those herds I had talked to about the rise."

"We sure did," Frank said and Ira agreed that they'd done it.

"Good, I'm going to get some sleep."

Ira told him that he'd put the horse up to go on.

He thanked Darling who nodded and smiled at him. He never expected that, but cooking for that crew had sure became her thing. Maybe she was like that before her sister ran off with her husband. He about chuckled out loud, recalling the too big of a dress incident. He'd never seen her since then that she wasn't nicely attired.

Before dawn, the breakfast triangle rang. He wasn't certain why with no cattle they were getting up so early, but his foremen had work for all the hands. Some of the men were settling down and breaking the rowdy horses, others fetching cooking wood to add to the mountain of it they'd started. There was plenty of work for all. One cowboy was on the roof replacing some bad shingles and using flattened tin cans in other spots to cure the roof leaks.

Rath liked the location and figured the rolling land was high enough not to flood. But when he went to check on the river later from a high point he saw the potential rising for a big one as the Arkansas spread out. It meant more delays in procuring stock.

Moving in a windmill was next. It would require several teams to pull it and some substantial running gear under it to make the trip. Ira had a map where the rig was at. Rath located several farmers with teams who'd help and he even found a large rimmed wagon he decided he could rent to move it on. Friday morning early they took their teams and joined the others at a cross road. Cowboys with horses lowered the rig on the running gears and with four teams they moved the mill to the ranch in six hours. All set up on the pads they'd poured, the mill was raised up again in place with little struggle. Bolted down, everyone went around clapping each other on the back about the great job they'd done. Darling had set out a feast of wild turkey and venison, potatoes, and beans they ate like starved wolves. And then she served them peach cobbler out of a Dutch oven. He thought a farmer or two who ate with them was ready to trade his wife for her. Each man was paid with a slip for the amount to be collected at McDonald's Bank

Ira promised the mill would be producing water in two working days. The next Monday they planed to move a large iron water tank down from Newton to set up. That evening as a bonus, Rath gave the hands two dollars apiece to run down to the Crossing on Saturday night since they'd gotten so much done—still no cattle from across the river. He rode home that night.

Their reunion was a sweet as he figured it would be. The next morning with him and her in a tight cocoon sleeping hard, he awoke to someone in the yard shouting his name before the sun came up. "Rath

Macon! Rath Macon! Marshal Cone's been shot. They need your help."

Chapter 14

"What will you have to do?" she hissed as they hurriedly dressed in the dark bedroom.

"I have no idea. I'll need to see about the situation and who did it. If they ran off then I may need to chase them down."

"Oh, dear God, don't they have any one to do that besides you?"

"Mary Ann, I have no idea. But I wouldn't be one bit surprised if the shooter hasn't ran off."

"Let them send someone else."

"I'll do what I have to do when I get there."

"Oh, I don't know what I'd do if I lost you now."

"I don't intend for that to happen."

"I am sure neither did he."

"I'll be fine, Stop worrying. I'm going to ride into town and see what happened."

He caught her and pulled her to him. "Easy, easy, I'll be fine. You can come in if you want to. But Cone is a friend of mine and whoever shot him needs to be brought to the law."

"I'm sorry." She leaned into his arms. "Be careful. I don't think I could face life without you."

'I'll harness your horse."

"No, go ahead. I can do that. But please don't leave until I get there?"

"I won't."

The excited man in the yard was Ab Hilton who accompanied him to the barn. "There were two of them.

They held up the store and were coming outside when Cone tried to stop them."

"Who were they?" he asked catching her horse.

"Two men is all I know. Never heard any names. They sent for the county Sheriff Bill Barlow to come down from Sanders, but he won't get there I bet till afternoon. McDonald said, for me to get you. He sent another man to your camp down south. He wasn't sure where you were at."

"Alright, put the harness on her horse while I saddle Red.'

"Sure, sure."

"No idea who the robbers were?"

"I never heard, but they can probably tell you all about them."

His horse saddled, he heard her coming from the house. He met her head on and stopped her. "Easy, I'll wait for you in town. Don't run that poor horse in the ground."

"I won't. I'm sorry that I got so hysterical."

He kissed her and loaded her in the buggy. With her set to go, he smiled at her in the predawn light. Then he did a leap on Red and tore out for Cherrydale. Whoever shot Cole was getting away.

McDonald waved him down in the street when he reached town. "Boy," he said to a young bystander. "Lead those two horses till they dry. Cone's upstairs in Doc's office"

"Who were the shooters?" Rath handed the youngster his reins

"Cone said Lawton Helpern was one of them and some other guy who wore an eye patch. They held up Roark at the store about ten o'clock last night. Several folks were in town late last night to shop. He was closing up real late for him, putting money away in the safe when they busted in with their guns in hand."

They were at the top of the stairs by then and McDonald was out of breath.

"One of them rode a bay horse, the other a chestnut with a scared face."

"Where is the county sheriff?" Rath opened the door and walked in doctor's office that smelled of ether.

"Aw, hell, he won't be here till noon."

A busty, gray haired women came in the room making a sign with her finger to her lip for them to be quiet.

"Is Marshal Cone asleep?" McDonald asked.

"Yes, he hasn't slept much either."

"Rath needs to talk to him."

She shook her head. "It will just have to wait."

"Is he still alive?" Rath asked.

McDonald nodded and they went out the door. headed down for the store.

"Which way did they go?"

"West I guess." The banker shook his head.

They went in the open front door and hurried to the back room. McDonald waving away a young clerk with, "We need to see him."

"He's in his office."

Rath and the banker found McGregor who looked sleepy, but he raised up at their entrance.

"Good, they found you." He rose to shake Rath's hand.

"Tell me all you can about them," Rath said.

"Halpern is six-three or four, big man. He had a five day beard and wears a gold ring on his left hand. Vest and pull over shirt, road floured. He has a scar on his left cheek—yeah, left side. The one eyed guy, he called Jules looked like a rat, pointed nose and some long whiskers in a sorry mustache like a rat would have. He had a double action pistol."

"Any idea where they were going to go?"

"Newton I figure and then beyond."

"Glad you weren't hurt. I'm surprised he shot Cone and that he didn't get a shot off."

"He shot at them. But they were behind their horses."

"What color horses did they escape on?"

"A chestnut and a bay."

"Thanks?" He knew that but wanted to be certain. Besides the man might have seen something different that the others missed

"What are you going to do next?"

"When my wife gets here I am going after them. They said the sheriff wouldn't get here till noon time."

McGregor agreed. "He probably won't."

Rath went outside and his wife came in a hard trot up to the porch and reined in her horse at the sight of him. "How is he?"

"Sleeping. A very tough women ran us off from the doctor's office. But I have a description of the robbers and I'm going to Newton and see if I can find them."

"Will they stop there?"

"They have money. The sin spots in Newton will be glad to liberate them of iHe nodded.

"I have thought about it and knew all along you would. I'll be here when you return or I can come to your aid if you need me." Her down look saddened him like a knife stuck in his guts.

"Thanks. I must do this."

"I'd be disappointed if you didn't feel that way. May God look out for you."

He kissed her good bye and went to tell McDonald what he had to do.

At the front door, the banker came out and nodded to Mary Ann who was beside him, then shook his hand. "Be careful. we have lots riding on our deal,"

"I'll be back shortly." When he started to turn the man caught him and handed him a roll of folding money. "You'll need this before it's over. Wire me if you run out. Anything needs to be done at the Crossing?"

"No. They can handle it. High as the water is, they won't be able to cross it for several days."

He hugged her quick like, stepped off the board walk, then swung on Red and rode northwest, waving at her. He heard McDonald tell her, *you've got a good man there*, before he set Red into a hard lope.

Late afternoon in Newton, he checked the stables, talked to the hustlers and owners. No one had stabled a one eyed man's horse that day nor even seen one. He didn't like that news—no one at the cross roads he'd spoke to along the way had either. He was doubting on his haunch to ride up there.

Shortly after that he left Red at Clover Dale stables, and walked the boardwalk for the Red Rooster Saloon where he knew a few people, he stopped a marshal in a black suit.

"My name's Macon. I live up at Cherrydale. Two men robbed a general store up there last night. I'm looking for them—the most likely one of the two you might have seen was short and one eyed"

The lawman shook his head. "What was his name?"

"Jules and he rode with Lawton Helpern."

"Never heard of them, sorry. How much money did they get?"

"Several hundred."

"Check the whorehouses. That's probably where they went first."

Rath thanked them and went on to the Red Rooster and ordered a beer. "Curly around?"

The barkeep nodded. "Yeah, he's gone to get a keg of beer."

"Fine, "Rath said and looked over the crowd in the room.

"He should be right back," the man said, delivering the mug piled in foam and took his dime.

Curly, a bald headed man in his forties came over and shook his hand. "Howdy Macon. I heard you've moved up here?"

"I'm living at Cherrydale."

The man in the apron across the bar nodded. "And you married some outlaw's widow."

"Great lady. I'm looking for a one eyed short guy named Jules."

"Don't know him."

"A big guy called Lawton Halpern?"

"A great big, foulmouthed trouble maker. I know him from Abilene. But I've not noticed him lately in here."

"Those two robbed the general store in the town up there last night. Shot the town marshal."

"Start checking the whore houses. Those kind go there first."

"Thanks. I need a good lead on them. I'll check back later with you."

"Sure, Macon. Good to see you. You got cattle up here already?"

"No and the Arkansas River is bank-to-bank so they're still south of here."

"Damn we could sure stand some business." He made a swipe at the scarred bar top with a towel. "I'll be here."

Rath downed the rest of the mug. Beer didn't taste that good to him anymore. "Appreciate you."

Then he left. There were four tents containing houses of ill repute in a row when he came outside the Rooster. The first one was Louise's. He noticed the wind had increased and over the loud music wafting out in the street, he could hear distant thunder. The tents sure popped a lot too. There'd be a storm up there before the night was over.

In Louise's parlor, several of the women jumped up at the sight of him. He shook his head and they slumped back down on the dusty looking sofas that formed the main room.

"What may I do for you?" the haughty woman in charge asked, hurrying over toward him with her cleavage propped up and shaking in the low cut front of her red silk dress.

"I'm looking for a short man wears an eye patch and a big man with a scar on his face."

The woman shook her head and frowned at the seated ones. "He's looking for two men—one has an eye patch the other a big man with a scar on his face."

"Ha," one of the frizzy headed one said and stood up. "Are you after Lawton?"

'Yes, have you seen him."

"Not recently. But Cookie you know him."

The heavier set one nodded, re-crossed her thick legs and made a face. "I ain't missed him either."

"I guess we are no help," the madam said. "What did they do?"

"Robbed a store and shot the town marshal."

"Bad men. But if you have few minutes any of my ladies would be more than glad to entertain you."

"No, thanks. I better check some more places."

Her hand familiarly on his shoulder as she showed him to the front flap. "I hate these damn tents in a storm and we may sure get one tonight. I'll be glad when we get to the river down there. Maybe I can have a real building then. These dumb farmers don't know how much money they will lose."

He thanked her again and she nodded. "Don't forget Louise's."

The occupants of next three pleasure palaces hadn't seen hide nor hair of the two either. Still determined he tried a few gambling centers but they had few customers and no one had seen the two men he described.

Weary of his dead end job he went back by Curly to check.

"Someone said he might be at Elton. Helpern has a wife or concubine there or did have."

"Where is that?"

"North of here on the cattle trail and west up the Blue River. That's the best directions I can give you. Just a small settlement."

"Good, I'll go check that out. Thanks." He put a half dollar on the bar for the man.

"Thanks."

'He ain't up there. I'll need you to try to find out anything you can about him. If I don't find him. I'll be back."

In his bedroll, he slept in the hay at the stables. Before dawn, he saddled Red and went to find breakfast. He found a tall blond headed woman in a white apron working a counter.

"Eggs, ham, and biscuits," he ordered, looking at others plates of men busy eating breakfast before they went to work.

"You the start of the damn cowboys?" she asked.

"No, I'm ahead of the wave."

She curled her lip. "Damn, I thought they might be close. Your food will be right out"

He thanked her. What was his wife doing? He missed being with her. He'd missed her the night before as well. In turn, he learned little in the café, finished his food and left Newton,

At the river, he rode the small rope powered ferry to cross. The Blue was up too. He could see the mounting storm hanging in the northwest. Dark ominous clouds piled higher and higher like the Rocky Mountains, he'd be glad to find this place of his before the storm struck—but the time left before the bad weather struck grew shorter.

Even the toothless old man who powered the ferry shook his head. "There's gonna be a bad one in here any minute."

The storm still held its position when he reached the Elton Store. But the air felt dead. Even the wind laid. He hitched Red and went inside. How much further? He spoke to the women behind the counter,

"Ma'am, I'm looking for Lawton Helpern."

"You're close. If he's home, his place is a mile west and a half mile north. You can't miss the turn off. It's at the foot of a hill and there's some big cottonwoods there. His place is on the right, oh, a quarter mile or so north of that."

"Thanks. Will his wife be home if he isn't?"

"You mean that girl he keeps?"

"I guess." He had no idea

"Her name's Iris. She won't be much help. Good luck."

"Have you seen him in the last few days?"

The woman shook her head. He could read by the expression on her face that she had not missed him either.

"He owe you money?" she asked.

"No. Is he hard to collect from?"

She laughed aloud. "You'll be lucky if you ever get it."

He nodded that he heard her. The thunder rattled some glass bottles on the shelves. Her shoulders gave a shutter. "You want to come hide in my cellar. I'm closing up this store, right now."

"No, but thank you." He followed her to the front door and she locked up behind him.

A swift shot of wind about took his hat off his head. After recovering it, he shook loose his slicker and put it on. Her cellar might have been a good place to wait out this storm. He jogged the anxious acting Red to the turnoff in the road she'd mentioned. Started north as rain began. Then pea-sized hail rolled off his shoulders and thudded on his hat.

There was fixing to be a real storm. Day turned to night and the rush of cooler air swept his face. Thunder broke over his head and deafened him. If he had any chance to catch him this storm might have cooped up Helpern at home.

The force on top of him began to roar in his ears like a freight train was about to swallow him. Rain turned to a flood pouring down on him and Red. The sulfur stink of the lightening burned his nostrils.

He wished to hell he'd accepted her generous offer of the cellar. At the moment, how he'd survived was his main wonderment. And the thunder became so close and fierce he wasn't certain he'd ever see Mary Ann again

Then it turned to a hard rain and he rode on sure-footed Red went up the sloping road hock deep in flooding water. He soon could make out a vague image of a far away house. Was it his? Was he home? God only knew. In the yard full of trash, wrecked wagons and junk he made the small porch grateful for the shelter. He knocked and looked back at his hipshot horse in the torrential downpour.

"Get in here." Some short woman grabbed him by the wrist and pulled him inside the dark interior and was pulling him further inside. All she wore was an old army blanket draped over her shoulders and obviously even in the shadowy light and flashes of lightening that was all she had on.

In the bedroom, she flung it off and held out a very white palm. She looked five-six. Maybe part Indian. Her bobbed black hair was straight and he guessed her as a teenager.

"I get fifty cents. You can stay longer but I charge for that too." Hands on her tawny colored bare hips, she waited for his reaction.

"I only want your man Halpern. Is he here?"

She folded her arms over her bare breasts and shook her head. "You don't want to climb in the bed with me?"

"No."

"Damn. I figured anyone come out in this bad weather was horny as a goat."

"Is he here?"

"Who?"

"Your man? Halpern."

"No, he left last night."

"He coming back?"

"I doubt it."

"Why is that?"

"Cause he had money. He never comes back again till he's broke."

"Was Jules with him?"

The left side of her upper lip curled. "You want that rat too?"

"Yes."

"You the damn law or something?"

"Something."

She plopped her butt on the bed and shook her head in disgust. "Damn, oh damn."

"He say where he was going?"

"Hell, no, he never does."

"I'd pay you a dollar to tell me where I can find him."

"Why I'd laid for you for half that much."

"Where did he go?"

"Nebraska, Ogallala." She held out her hand and he paid her.

"Who does he know up there?"

She was kicking her short bare legs. "Some guy named Nettles."

"What does he do?"

She held out her palm again.

He paid her another dollar.

"He sells beef to the army and the Injuns. Now do you want me?" She looked up at him for an answer.

"No, ma'am."

"If I dress will you stay here and drink some coffee with me?"

"I guess."

"It's still raining like hell out there. You just as well." She stood on the bed and walked across it to get a dress off the bed post and put it on openly while he watched the flood on the small window panes.

"What else can you tell me about him?"

"He's got a whore in Ogallala,"

"What's her name?"

"Francis is all I know." Dressed at last, she yawned big, still standing on the bed. "That worth a dollar?"

He nodded,

"Damn if you're ain't *gonah* leave me a rich bitch."

"He got any other stops between here and there?' he asked as she stoked up the fire in the stove and put the water on to boil. She came over and sat down in a chair on her leg facing him and looking at him hard for any waver in his eyes.

"I ain't ugly, am I?"

"I don't think so."

"Good. You married?"

"Yes."

"I could have guessed that." She pushed the bobbed hair back from her face

"What else will he do or go see out there?"

"If I knew anything else that you would pay a dollar for I'd damn sure tell you."

"Who's place is this?"

"He says it was his." She shrugged. "I figure someday they'll come throw my ass out of the front door, huh?"

"I have no idea."

"You must be a cattle drover?"

"I was."

"What you do now?" She jumped up at the sound of water boiling and added some coffee grounds from a hand crank grinder's drawer.

"Buy cattle."

After he drank a cup of her brew, the rain let up outside and he rose to leave. She impulsively hugged him and then looked up. "Only other guy ever got out of here before without laying me was a preacher. Now there's two, huh?"

"Have a good day, Iris."

"Tell me your name again."

"Rath Macon."

"Got it. I hope the thunder quits. A cowboy I knew was kilt by one of them bolts."

"I'll try to avoid them."

"Good, You come see me you ever need a real woman."

Outside, he mounted Red and waved at her huddled under her blanket on the porch watching him leave. The rain had not completely quit and the temperature had dropped considerable. If he hadn't had such a lovely wife at home, he'd probably not made her list. Grateful to be on the move again, he considered riding north to catch the westbound train at York Nebraska and meet Halpern when he arrived in Ogallala.

Chapter 15

He caught the train in York, Nebraska. His horse Red was boarded with a farmer, he promised to be back in not over two weeks for him. He couldn't afford any more time away from his buying station. He telegraphed McDonald and Mary Ann where he was headed. At a roaring clicked-clack of rail joints at twenty-five miles an hour, he rolled west in a car seat shared with another man named O'Day who sold farm machinery.

The man talked about how good his business was across Nebraska selling dealers, plows, discs and wagons. He also had a mowing machine line and sold binders. In the spring time he sold baby chicks to stores.

"This state will be one of the top farming states in the nation in a short while. Looking out the window at the homesteads and sod houses, he had no doubt civilization was coming on the run.

Fifteen hours later he and hundreds of honyonkers dismounted the train in Ogallala. He shook the salesman's hand and wished O'Day good luck on his sales .

"I hope you catch those robbers too,"

So did he. He checked in the Grand Palace Hotel, then went to see the local sheriff. Tom Gravely was a large man, bald headed and his collar button was undone when he reached over the desk, shook his hand and offered him a seat.

"What brings you to Ogallala, Mr. Macon?"

"Rath. Two men robbed a general store in my town of Cherrywood, Kansas. They shot a close friend of mine, the town marshal and they are headed up here according to rumor."

"I can understand your concern. What are their names?"

"Lawton Halpern and a one eyed shorter man named Jules."

Gravely nodded with a smug set to his lips. "Jules La Blancke."

"I'm not sure of his last name, but obviously you know him?"

"They've been here before. When will they arrive?"

'If I knew that I'd be a gypsy fortune teller. I rode north and caught a train from York when I learned their destination."

"I have a warrant for both of them for previous crimes they committed here."

"Good then you can hold them."

"Yes, but they'll be careful since they know they're wanted here."

"Halpern has a woman named Francis. He did everywhere else too. Had a woman I mean."

The lawman nodded. "I don't know about Francis. The one I know is a teamster owns a freight line. Tough as rawhide and a real bitch. Her name's Bonnie Sherman. She could whip most men."

"I didn't think she would be some demure little woman." Rath chuckled at his image of the woman.

"She has a ranch north of town, but I'd be damn careful scouting around it."

"Thanks. If I may check back with you, I'll be glad to keep you informed about what I learn. Oh, his last woman mentioned a man called Nettles."

"New one on me. Good. Between the two of us, we may lock them up."

Rath agreed, rose and shook the man's hand. Things were different then he thought—Halpern was wanted there and that surprised him that he would plan to return. Perhaps he expected this Bonnie woman to keep him safe. No telling, he needed to know more about her business.

After a bath and a shave, in late afternoon, he began to visit bars looking for prospects of men he might hire or bribe them to keep him informed about Halpern's return. If he even came there. There was lots of country between there and Kansas for him to get lost in. Maybe he'd made a mistake in his haste to come this far on the word of some strange woman called Iris.

No time to doubt his methods or decisions, he met a teamster at the Wild Horse Saloon. A noisy place with wild gambling going on at tables and lots of tough men hoisting thick glass mugs of beer. And plenty of slutty bar maids flashing views of their breasts for tips as they served the customers. The place stirred in wild bedlam and talking was hard to hear over the raucous sound levels,

"Helpern? Aye, I know the bastard. He ain't been around since last fall."

"All I want to know is where he is at."

The big man nodded. "Not a word who told yah? If I see him."

"Not a word who told me."

The man nodded. "I'll leave word at the hotel and you can give Mike behind the bar here me money."

They shook hands. Rath thanked him. Money always talked. Of course he could also run to Bonnie and tell her about the Texan looking for her love interest. But he doubted she'd pay him five bucks for the news. He also didn't know any Nettles either.

In the morning, he rented a horse to look over her operation. He spent that evening looking for and finding some other drovers he knew from the past like Tad Holden. A man in his fifties with a bad limp. His beard gone gray, he smiled big at the sight of him.

"What in hell yeah doing up here this time of year?" The man blinked his blue eyes in disbelief.

"Do you have all night?" Rath asked.

"Damn right."

He told him a summary of coming home to a sellout and divorce.

The man shook his head. "I'd of killed her."

No doubt the tough old man might have done that. Then he told him about the store robbery and his friend being shot.

"I need a friend like you. Tell me about the two robbers."

He told him what he knew about Halpern and his cohort. The man nodded. "I'll keep an eye out for them."

"Thanks. I'm staying at the hotel across the street."

He turned in about midnight and was up eating breakfast when the clock in the café struck seven am. The chubby waitress left him a twenty-five cent bill for his food on the counter and smiled. "Have a good day."

"Thanks." His mind was on Mary Ann at home and how much better he would feel facing her over his plate of eggs, bacon, fried potatoes and toast.

His ride out to the woman's ranch proved little. Her house and corrals were a quarter mile of waving grass from the road. So without invading her place, he had little chance of seeing much of anything.

He loved the rolling country and all the grass he rode over. Good cow country but right against the reservations of the Sioux and they were long from becoming settled. He stopped at a small cross roads store and bought a sandwich made from beef sausage and home made bread.

The store keeper took his dime and thanked him. "You must be from Texas?"

"I was, but live in Kansas now."

"What brought you up here?"

"Looking for two outlaws who shot a friend

The man nodded he'd heard him. "Who are they?"

"Lawton Halpern's one."

The man looked around to be certain they were alone. "He's coming."

Rath frowned at him in shock. "You know that he's coming?"

He wet his lower lip and acted as if he'd became restrained before he finally said, "Halpern's a mean cruel man. I'd killed him for how he mistreated my wife one day in this store last time he was up here. But I can't hit a barn with a gun. Yesterday I overheard Bonnie say to one of her men in here that he'd be up here soon."

"The sheriff wants him too. Good. Keep your ear to everything. You can send me a message at the Palace Hotel. I won't tell a soul."

"Good. I hope you get him."

Confident, he rode the plain rental horse back to Ogallala. He stopped at the sheriff office and told him what he'd learned. The man nodded. "That's good. We'll get him. Good detective work."

Back at the hotel, the clerk handed him a note from Holden. *I learned last night Halpern is coming here. Good luck.* All he had to do was find out how and where he would land.

He sent McDonald and Mary Ann each a telegram about where he was at and that he was close to getting his man. The next two days drug by and no Halpern. Then his teamster left him a note at the hotel. *Halpern arrived at her place last night Pay Harry.*

First he went to find the sheriff, but he was out. The clerk only said he wasn't there, but should return by dark.

"Does he have an undersheriff?"

"He's taking a prisoner to Denver this week. What can I do?"

"When he returns tell him Macon has news."

"I will, sir." He left and gave the fiver to Harry and had a beer. The wait on the sheriff would not be easy to stand. He finally gave up and went to bed at the hotel. Sometime in the night, Sheriff Gravely knocked on his door.

"I'm sorry to wake you. I had to serve some papers. Where is he?"

"My man said he was at her ranch."

"I'll gather a posse, get a search warrant and we'll ride up there at seven am."

"When you getting any sleep?"

"Sheriffs don't need sleep. Didn't you know? I'll tell the desk clerk to wake you at 6 am. See you then."

Scratching the hair on top of his head, Rath watched him head for the staircase down the dim lit hallway. Alright, they'd do something in the morning. He closed the door.

The sheriff was there at the livery though he looked haggard. Six men armed with rifles rode out to arrest the pair. Their horses' hooves drummed on the great bridge across the Platte River. It was rain swollen too. Local farmers and ranchers rode in the posse. A friendly bunch, but Rath could see there were no fools in the crowd. A few asked what he did and he told them, he bought culls and shaped them up.

One man nodded. "I'd never thought of that, but I bet it works."

"I need to get back down there too. Hope we find these two."

Two men who knew the way went in the back way to her place and the sheriff gave them some time to get in place. Then the four rode up the lane with Rath. Her stock dogs were barking full force. A tall buxom woman came out of the house in a brown dress. She must have stood six feet or more, Rath decided. She might be his age and she didn't look pleased to see the sheriff who dismounted.

"What the fuck do you want Gravely?"

"Two men. Lawton Helpern and Jules."

'They ain't here." She stomped her bare foot on the porch floor.

"I have a search warrant."

"You ain't coming in my house."

"Tell them two to come out here, then."

"Tell you to stick it up your ass."

"You've got two minutes and woman or not I'm coming in."

'My men will shoot you."

"Not if they want to live. I am the law in this county."

Rath wondered who'd win. She was tough acting as any man. Then a shot broke the silence and with spurs he drove his livery horse around the house. In time to see the shooter facing the two posse members coming in from behind, he slid the horse to a stop and raised the rifle to his shoulder. "Drop it!"

The hard faced man whirled and Rath cut him down with a quick shot. The shorter men raised his hands. The other two deputies dismounted and thanked him. Rath still shaken some, searched around for any more opposition.

The sheriff came charging through the house and busted out the back door. "Everyone alright?"

"Except for Halpern," Rath said.

One of the posse men was on his knees checking on him. "He should live. He wouldn't put his gun down and Macon shot him."

"Thanks," Gravely said. He turned to the red faced woman who pushed by to get to Halpern. "You're under arrest too, ma'am."

"What the hell for?"

"All the untaxed whiskey kegs in your living room."

"Well, gawdamn you, Gravely!" She spoke to Halpern. "We'll get you to the doctor, darling. You'll be fine."

"When he gets out of the Kansas pen," Rath said, shoving the rifle in his scabbard.

"You Kansas law?" she asked, her lip curled in a snarl.

"No, but he shot a Kansas marshal back there."

Gravely put handcuffs on her and sat her down on the steps, then he ordered a flunky worked for her to hitch a wagon up to take them and the whiskey to town in. Shaking his head at her bitching and cursing, he told the others that they'd needed to load the untaxed whiskey as evidence in the wagon too.

"You ever need work," he said to Rath. "Come see me. You're a tough hand at this business. I could sure use you out here."

"Thanks. I plan to catch the first train east and get back. I've got a business to run. I'll let Kansas law extradite him. You'll hear from them."

"Ride easy," Gravely said and the others shook his hand.

By evening he'd wired the folks at home the news, and then sat on the late passenger train headed east for York and Red. He slept some sitting up on the bench seat. But the swaying train about made him so sick to his stomach he quit that and sat arms folded dozing off.

He slept a few hours in the hay at the farmer's place who had taken care of Red. He'd paid him. However the man's wife stopped Rath from leaving and fed him motherly like.

Four long days later him and his exhausted horse rode in the yard and got off to pet the half crazy dogs who were jumping around him for his attention. Good to see them. Then she burst out of the house and ran to hug him.

"Ohm honey, I'm so damn dirty."

'Who cares? You're home and alright." She smothered his whisker bristled face with kisses.

"I'm going to strip naked and wash out here." He looked around.

"No one's here. I'll go get some soap and a towel."

Before he could stop her, she was gone after bath things for him. He unsaddled Red and put him in the lot. The grateful gelding laid down and rolled in the dirt, while Rath unbuckled his gun belt and began to undress. In minutes she returned. He took a pail from the barn and went to the great tank.

He dipped out a bucket and she poured it on him. It was not that warm, but he would be clean anyway. After bathing, he walked on tender soles, he carried part of his things and she bought the rest.

Her wheat was over waist high. He could hardly believe the size of it in the short time he'd been gone. But most of all he was with her again and where he belonged.

"Sorry I can't carry you inside."

"I'm not worried about that. I'm just glad you're back." She playfully shoved him up the stairs. "I'm not in any hurry but if you can run I'll keep up."

They ate supper after dark. Then slept in the next morning. It was noise of a crowd outside that woke him. He reached for his six gun, but decided they were revelers. And he rushed to put on his pants and shirt. She was already up dressing as well.

"Friends," he said and smiled. "They mean well."

"They could have waited a week." Then she laughed.

He went out on the back porch carrying his boots and socks.

"Morning." he said to the crowd and sat down to put on them on. "Nice to see you all."

"Better to see you are alright," Cone said walking up. His arm in a sling. "We couldn't wait to congratulate you. Our spies said you'd ridden home last night."

"Whew, you've been all over the world," McDonald said, getting out of his rig. "And caught those outlaws." That drew a cheer.

"And it's damn good to be back in this corner of Kansas." He hugged her to his side. "I didn't do much, but the sheriff wanted those men arrested up there on charges he has and he'll let Kansas have them when he gets through. We took a posse and went to his lady friend's place with a warrant and arrested them."

"Did you have to shoot one of them?"

"Yeah, he wouldn't put his gun down. Just did my job."

"You're getting good at that," McDonald said. "You sure made the Nebraska newspapers. We simply wanted to thank you for all you've done and tell you the river's gone down some and your men are handling the buying."

Good news. They were handling it.

He shook hands with lots of folks and they headed back to town. She hustled up some breakfast and he dressed for church.

"There's lots of good folks in Kansas," she said.

He agreed. "We've got time to make church."

"Yes, we better go." She smiled at him with their coffee poured. Then she slipped in a seat across from him. "Your face sure looks good over there to me."

"I couldn't be prouder than to have you."

She agreed and they ate. Lots of folks would ask him questions at church but he had lots to be thankful for.

Chapter 16

Monday morning early he rode for the river. He still felt tired but that too would catch up when he got back in a routine. She planned to join him at the end of the week. He rode Rebel and figured on using the gray some after he got there. Folks were busy planting corn in the bottom land. The small tree leaves were opening up fast. It was time the early herds got up there.

He discovered two small herds of cattle grazing when he reached the cow camp. One bunch of sore footed ones and a mixed herd of cows and young cattle, the process was working. Close to noon time by then, he found Darling doing dishes up to her elbows in suds.

"We heard you got them outlaws?"

He dropped out of the saddle. "They're in the Ogallala jail."

"My daddy always said you need a job done don't send a boy. Course he never had no boys so us girls had to do it all."

She stripped the suds off her forearms and went to get him some coffee. "Things here went pretty good while you were gone. They hired a few more cowboys to hold things together. Ira's gone to get some more today."

"How is Darling getting along?"

"Hell, boss man, just fine. I have had three proposals of marriage since I took this job." She bent over and poured him a cup of coffee.

When he accepted it with a nod, he asked, "You have any plans?"

"Lord, no. I like this job. Most parts of it are just right for me."

"If I find a helper would you like that?"

"I reckon. Keep adding hands this might get to be a bitch for me to handle."

He nodded and listened to the circling red tail hawk overhead "telling him to leave." They were pretty protective of their territory and his screams of protest were shrill. They'd even take on a bald eagle and there were several of them up and down the Arkansas River.

"We'll see what I can find. No fights? No wrecks?" He sipped on the coffee and listened.

"I tell you this is a peaceful bunch."

"Good. I'll ride back into town. Anything you need?"

She wet her lip. "I'd pay you, but a bar of lavender soap would be nice. This lye soap is rough on my hide."

"I can do that." He dropped his empty cup in the washtub, then went and caught his grazing horse. Frank must have seen him he was riding in.

"Good to have you back in one piece."

"They're in the Nebraska jail."

"I figured so, being back this soon." Frank dismounted and shook his hand. "We've bought some. Had to yoke a couple wild ones but it's going good. Ira's gone to the outfit comes from down by Austin. Flecker Brothers, I think. They know you he said. They've got maybe forty limpers to cut out."

"That might be alright. I know lots of those guys when I see them. But there is no telling. You got some new men."

"We're just hiring the good ones." He sounded all most defensive.

"Hey, you two know as much as I do about cowboys. Any man has to prove himself."

"I know. We've been real picky."

"We should be. Talk more later. I'm going to town. I see the windmill's pumping."

"We've got a few hands could build a factory. We have three showers under tubs that the sun heats."

"Sounds better than a muddy creek to wash up in."

"Hey, right and with her great cooking, we're living high on the hog."

Rath agreed and headed for the Crossing. Things would get busy from there on. When he rode up at the distance he saw already some large tents were springing up around the few permanent buildings. Hammers were ringing out and hand saws cut fresh smelling lumber. The race was on for building the new railhead with workers scurrying like ants to get the frames up in the sky.

He found Harry busy in the Texas saloon and ordered some stew. In her better outfit; she served him and smiled. "You ain't been in here much lately."

"I went to Nebraska to arrest some outlaws."

"That sounds exciting."

"It wasn't that big a deal. Say I need a teenage boy to be my cook's helper."

She nodded. "I can send one to see you. His name is Yodder."

"Yodder who?"

She turned up her palms. "I don't know. But he will work."

"Send him to my cow camp."

"I will. He needs work real badly."

"I can use him if he'll work."

She nodded and rushed off.

He ate his stew, paid Harry and went outside on the porch.

Two ramrod looking guys rode up and they looked familiar hitching their horses.

"Why Dan, look there is that Rath Macon," the older one said to his partner.

"Hey Macon, you are a sight for my sore eyes. Elliot Corning and my brother Wash. Remember us?"

"You boys are from west of Waco?"

"That's us, we've been hearing about you since we crossed the Canadian. You're buying culls?"

"You boys got a herd?"

"Have we got a herd, Wash?" he asked his brother.

"Yeah and we got several culls. What do you pay?"

"Eight dollars a head for ones I can use."

"We'll buy you a drink, come on in."

"Fine." These boys would know the cull market in the past. It shouldn't take long to convince them.

He'd nursed a beer the whole time and they were well into a bottle of whiskey after an hour of talking business, cattle prices and them extracting the story of his foreclosure sale. They promised to have a culling on the north shore of the Arkansas and he told them to tell Harry at the Texas Saloon and he'd get the word. He took the ferry across the river and learned his foreman Ira was five miles south with the Four H bunch talking business.

Late afternoon he joined Ira and Sam Springer at his camp. The older man got up stiffly and shook his hand. "Good to see you again. Glad that damn hussy didn't put you down for long."

Why he'd almost forgotten her. They talked about the cattle prices and what was happening in Newton. Springer said he had his share of culls and would cut them out on the north bank for them. Ira nodded at Rath who agreed. His foreman was doing good at this job.

All Rath could see ahead was they'd be busy for some time. McDonald came down the next week in his buggy and looked over their growing herd. He and Rath rode the country inspecting the purchases, several of the cows and heifers had even dropped calves in that bunch. There would be more.

"What do you think?' Rath asked.

"You're doing exactly what you said you'd do and I'm impressed. Will these limpers recover?'

Rath nodded. "Most of them will. Some have too much wrong and we can eat them when they gain some weight. I think we can sell some to local butchers too. What do you know about Indian suppliers of meat down in the Indian territory?"

"I always heard it was a buy yourself a market. Lot of hands under the table deals." McDonald frowned.

"I'll do some checking. We might could deliver some beef down there that wouldn't make the big market up here."

The banker laughed. "I hadn't even thought of that. Did you figure that out going to Nebraska?"

"Maybe riding that train back and forth." Rath shook his head amused. He'd never live down that story about his ride up there figuring out this cull business.

McDonald approved everything, wished him luck and then drove home that night.

Rath was drinking coffee after supper with the crew. They'd yoked two pair of two year olds that were wild that day. Frank mentioned they might have been in the big herd cause they couldn't cull them out originally.

"I've shot some like that and we ate 'em," Ira said. "First cattle I brought up to Abilene in '67 they had not been handled until someone caught them out of the brush, cut and branded them. They'd only seen a man one time and they were wilder than damn deer. They stampeded every night on us. A cricket farted and they ran off. Cattle today even the full blood longhorns ain't near as bad as then. 'Course some are that way naturally."

"You'd been wild too, if someone cut you, notched your ear and then branded you."

Another rider said, "We caught them at night. They laid up in the tough brush all day."

Even, Rath recalled doing that after he came home from war and made his decision to gather cattle. Those cattle were wilder then but many were seven-eight years old and had been running free all of their life. Many herds had six to seven feet horn spans. Those real wild cattle were about all gone by then. Durham blood began to speckle them, but he didn't miss them crazy ones and the wrecks they'd caused.

"They run some pretty crooked games in the Crossing." one man complained.

"Don't go in them places and gamble," Rath said. "They're all crooks. Charlie Goodnight fired his best foreman for gambling and him getting the word back to him."

"Fighting or gambling, either one will get you fired at his place."

"I ain't that fussy," Rath said. "Are you Darling?"

She shook her head, drying her dishes. "Hell, yeah got to have some excitement in a cow camp. Get pretty boring after while." Then she laughed. "Just don't fight around the cook's space."

"There is a boy coming to do your dishes," Rath said, recalling his deal with Clair at the saloon. "His name is Yodder."

She nodded and never said another word. He'd recalled the soap and earlier she thanked him for filling her request. He couldn't get over her improved appearance and recovery from the woman he bought the wagon from. She really did enjoy the cowboys and the rest of it. But she was full step up from the tough talking bitch he thought he had hired.

Why those hands would lay down their lives for her. How many proposals had she gotten? That was almost funny, but they hadn't seen her sister yet either.

He spend his days in the saddle visiting herds, arranging cullings and working cattle at the headquarters. His herd had grown soon to a thousand and they were working west but the grass was growing. Additions by the week soon ran fifty or more a day.

One man came by and asked what Rath'd take for his cow and calf pairs. He said a hundred bucks a pair and the guy blinked his eyes at the price, but two days later he was back offering eighty five. Frank promised him there were a hundred head. They agreed on ninety bucks apiece for the pairs and he'd take all if they'd put his brand on them.

Rath sold them and told him to go pay McDonald for a hundred head, he could pay for anymore he got on delivery.

McDonald came out the next morning, must have gotten up before dawn and driven down there. His first question was, *How many more pairs do we have now?*

"Maybe a dozen, but we'll have more."

"Whew, that 100 head sale pays for everything and then some. You want your money now?"

Rath shook his head. "We'll have more later."

"That was nine thousand dollars. Nearly all the money we have in the rest of them" MacDonald acted excited. "Oh, I've talked to a man sells the Indian agencies cattle. He's interested. Pays twelve cents a pound dressed for them delivered down in the Territory."

"I think we need more money than that for carcass beef. That's about a seventy dollars for a big steer," Rath said. "I want eighty or ninety." But some of these cripple steers that might not mend but they will fatten not being driven all over?"

"Can we butcher them and make money," MacDonald said

"I think we can. We've got some great workers. But this cow deal is better than I even imagined."

The banker smiled. "You told me we'd make money."

Rath nodded. "That guy couldn't of bought those cows at Newton and got them branded. There is a price to pay for convenience. Besides those cowboys have to kill them or leave the calf and cow behind. We have some dry cows lost their calves on the way up here that will fatten this summer.

"Damn, you did think long and hard about this deal and setup." McDonald shook his head in amazement.

McDonald had a special breakfast that Darling set up for him when she discovered he had not eaten in hours. She fussed enough about him even opening a fresh can of condensed milk just for his coffee. *That other might be getting stale,* she said.

Besides having her hair all up in a neat bun and wearing her best white blouse. The brown skirt she wore, swung like willow tree limbs in a soft wind with her moving about camp. Rath noted his partner made a good check on her moving about getting him setup and before he left, he said, "She made a real cook, didn't she?"

Rath agreed. Yodder arrived on the ranch wagon bringing supplies for her and he reported to Rath.

"I'd come sooner on foot , but they told me this was rattle snake breeding season out here and if I didn't have high tops boots they'd bite me for sure. So I waited to catch a ride on your wagon."

"Let's go meet your boss." He was about to bust out laughing over the sincere rattlesnake story, but he contained it.

"Darling, this is Yodder. He comes from back east somewhere and he'd been here sooner, but the *cowboys* told him this was rattlesnake breeding season and he'd get bit walking out here without high top boots."

She swallowed her amusement, straightened her back and without a smile said. "We don't let them breed on this ranch. Go fetch me two pails of water and then we can heat it."

Him out of hearing, she broke down, bent over laughing until she cried. *Rattle snake breeding season.*

"I'm glad you–you don't let them do that out here." Rath was completely gone to his own laughter.

Yodder was his new man. Dressed in some real patched up overalls, he looked like a poor bum. She found him some better clothes and borrowed better ones from the others then she cut his wild blonde hair and made him part of the outfit. The boys even taught him how to ride in the evenings.

Herd culling became an everyday item for his crews. His wife came in three day spells to stay in the side wall tent and they had some private times together, but Mary Ann understood her husband's business required his attention through the next few months when eighty percent of the herds would come north.

She met lots of his drover friends and listened to the deals he made selling healed limpers by the Fourth of July for full price. Seated in the quiet night air on cots in his tent, with the occasional bawling of cattle in the back ground.

"They will bind my wheat next week and the thrasher crew is coming," she told him.

"That late already?" He studied her nod. "Will you need help?"

"No, but I'll have to feed the harvesters so I probably won't be able to come down next week."

'Then I'll come up and we can go to the social on Saturday night."

"But your work here?"

"Ira can handle things. We've hire four more hands and bought forty more horses for the men."

She jumped up and tackled him on the cot. "That would be wonderful."

"Wait till I close down the tent," he whispered. "This tent is obviously way too open."

"Oh, I'm sorry." She struggled up then and went to close the north tie back, while he did the south. Next she blew out the candle lamp, then they raced to get undressed and onto one cot. He hoped their impulsive honeymoon never stopped.

Later listening to some coyotes howl, he snuggled to her warm bare back and half asleep dreamed of being

back at her place where they had the place to
themselves.

Cattle kept coming north and his herds
increased. Proctor, the cow buyer, came back and
bought more cow/calves. He planned to take them
north in the spring to western Nebraska. One winter in
Kansas, killed the tick fever they spread. Along with
some red durham bulls he bought in Illinois to cover
them, he had them up on the Republican River Country
north of Abilene. And his men was busy stacking hay up
there.

Rath sold several bunches of healed limpers on
the Newton market and began to cut out steers that still
limped but were fat. They might limp all the rest of their
lives. He was two-four days hard driving from any
reservation down in the territory. How could he get the
meat down there and it not spoil?

He'd been selling butchered cattle up in Newton.
But that was only a few at a time. A couple of his hands
became butchers and they could dress out a steer in no
time. He cut the price a cent or so under the going
market and did well. But getting them to any other
market quick enough was a problem; he found no
solution for it.

His wife had gone home and he promised her to
be home by Saturday so they could attend the dance.
They were culling the Starr Ranch herds out of Uvalde
on the north side of the Arkansas. Two herds of twenty
five hundred head per herd. It hadn't rained and it was
exceptionally dry right there. Dust boiled up. The cattle

didn't like it any better than the ranch hands doing the sorting.

Rath was with the holding herd on the west side. He rode the gray horse and he was a cutting fool—an angry cow came out of the dust looking for something to hook on her five foot horns. He hollered at a teenager keeping them close and then saw the boy hadn't heard him and he whirled Gray to chase her. Grabbing for his *reata,* he guided Gray with his knees but the cow pony knew in an instant that she was who he wanted.

He widened the loop, whirled it over his head and stood up to pitch it over her horns. His rope fell over them and he jerked slack with a back hand jerk, then raised the reins to turn her off. He dallied around the horn, she went left and the *reata* stretched. He gave some slack, then he put the rope over her hip and still in his turn, hit Gray with the spurs.

He flipped the cow on her back before her horn tips ever reached the retiring wide eyed cowboy and his cow pony. The *reata* broke and slapped Rath hard on the recoil on his hat and cheek. It hurt but the boy was alright

When the big cow got up, she staggered back in the dust to the herd. The young cowboy came back and asked if he was okay?

"Yes, go get me another lariat," he said with a smile. Things went better from there on the rest of that day.

The next morning he ate breakfast with the crew, ready to ride home. "I'll be back first of the week. This rush is about over. There will be less herds coming the next few weeks and then it will be about over.

"What happens then?"

"McDonald is talking about buying hay. Originally we were going to put cattle out to farmers but they aren't herders. Over by my wife's farm, there were a handful of draft horses loose for a year. No one could catch them. She and I got them in pens in half a day."

"Hay maybe cheaper than using them," Ira said.

"We will have to make a decision soon," Rath told them.

He rode home and when he came into sight he saw the bundled yellow sheathes in her fields. Hot air came out of the south on a fiery wind. The distant chug of a steam engine tractor in her neighbor's field told him thrashers were close by. Summer time in Kansas and his first summer at farming even at arms length.

From the house, she rushed out to met him. He stripped out his latigoes and stopped to kiss her. "How have you been?"

"Hot, but cool now that you're here."

He wiped his forehead on his sleeve. "That doesn't sound like anything I'm feeling. Except I'm glad to be back with you." Saddle put up, he went arm in arm with her to the house.

"We'll have to leave soon to make the social."

"No problem."

In an hour, they left for the social in her buggy. The sky from horizon to horizon was deep blue and he drove the horse in an easy trot to the schoolhouse. Nice to be back in her company, things went on he'd already made over ten thousand dollars for his part in the cull business. They needed to do good at this business, there would be several try to copy him next year. This would be the best season this operation would ever make.

"I'm glad you're here," She squeezed his arm. "I know you have lots of things down there that need you."

"No more than I need you."

They came over the rise and he could see the schoolhouse. His warm memories of the first time coming over the hill filled him with lots of good feelings about his second meeting with Mrs. Cates were then about to unfold here. He stopped at the steps for her to get out the food she'd prepared.

A hard faced man came out the schoolhouse door with his gun aimed at Rath. She screamed. Rath drew and fired, the man was hit. He went down on the porch but Rath couldn't see her. His heart stopped and he flew around the buggy. She was on the ground. Face down. No. Then he thought he saw her stir and there were some shots again. Not from the schoolhouse. Gun still in his hand, Rath saw through the veil of blue gun smoke another man in the saddle try to raise his gun. His shot cut him down.

He was on his knees beside her in deep concern. "Mary Ann?"

"I'm fine. I'm fine," she gasped. "I lost my wind when I fell on the dish."

Her alright, he shot to his feet. "Who in the hell is doing all this shooting?"

"Mr. Phillips shot the man on the horse who was going to shoot you," a boy said.

He knew Phillips from the bank robbery. He pointed at the man on the foot of the steps he'd shot. "Who was this man?"

"His name's Tell Kraft. He's one of the reb haters. A hard liner. They were holding all the women in the schoolhouse," a man in overalls said.

"When you got him," Phillips said. "I knew the women were alright inside and I went for my rifle in the wagon. I tried to stop him. He kept trying to shoot you. I had no choice."

"That's no problem." He helped Mary Ann to get on her feet, kissed her so grateful she was okay. The rest of the concerned women took her inside. Rath couldn't connect everything. Were these some more of those men that accused him of being with Bloody Bill Anderson?

"Kraft's dead," the older man said, who'd been down checking on his pulse and then stood up.

"Who was with him? The man Phillips shot?" Rath asked. Still shaking inside and out, he realized the two conspirators had taken control of the group there to get a chance to kill him. This had to stop. They could have hurt lots more people than simply him. The kids running around–those bastards were crazy.

"A guy named Vern Byers. Just a farmer."

"There is someone behind all this. Someone who sends these guys in and must tell them lies about my war record. Someone real sick. I'd never had been in

Kansas or anyplace else but Mississippi and Louisiana during the war."

The shootings dulled the spirit of the evening. A deputy sheriff was sought and he questioned everyone. The county coroner claimed the bodies. Cone also came out and talked to Rath.

"I thought we had this under control," the lawman apologized. "You've done more for folks in this county than any man living. I had no idea they planned to get you here."

"I hate worse the damn threat to the kids and women here." Rath was still upset.

Cone agreed. "We need to stop them."

"That boy they hired to follow me knows more than he's told us, I think."

"I'll question him in the morning. He said he only did that because he needed money. How is your wife."

"She's fine. I've spent some time with her tonight. She thought he'd shot me and I thought she'd been shot by him."

"We'll end this," Cone said. "Go keep her company."

Rath nodded. He joined her on the bench along the wall. "Things going better?"

"I guess I can't tell. I wanted this to be such a great evening for us."

"It is."

"What will it take to make these people believe the war is over?"

Rath shrugged. "They couldn't forget you were the outlaw queen."

"That just came on me."

"Well, I'm glad I have you any way."

She squeezed his hand and swallowed hard.

The drive home was quiet. He feared most that the damn trouble makers had broken up their honeymoon. In deep concern, he wanted that back. They reached her place in a stuffy summer night. Things he had to solve when the rush let up at the Crossing, he had to isolate the ring leader.

The buggy horse unhitched, she fell in his arms and cried. "I was never so scared in my life. I couldn't get my breath. I knew you were dead and shots were going off all over."

"Hey, let's forget it. I am here in one piece. Those boys ain't gong to bother us again." He swept her up in the susie bugs shrill night sounds and carried her to the house.

"It's you and me against them all."

She hugged his head and kissed him. "It's us. It's us, I love you so much."

Chapter 17

They went to church. He told her he felt they needed to go. She agreed. After breakfast, they drove the horse and buggy over there and joined the congregation in song and prayer. They spoke to many people and, as usual, her parents ignored them.

The thresher owner, Jim Crane introduced himself. "We'll be rolling your way Tuesday. Means we'll be set up to start threshing Wednesday."

She nodded. "My farmer told me to have lunch ready. I have two hard working young men who will be there to help you. Mr. Hanson will be there too. And lots of neighbors have promised to help us," she added.

"See you then, Mrs. Macon."

They went outside in the hot day and drove the buggy back home. The brown harvested wheat fields had turned the country rolling brown. Corn sheaves rustled in the south wind, but the ears were made and there would be a corn crop.

"Will the wheat crop pay your bills and taxes?" he asked, crossing the nearly dry creek that had been flooding only a few months earlier.

"It has been." The horse's hoofs thumping on the thick boards.

"We aren't in any danger, but do you owe for the farm?" he asked.

"No, he paid for it, I guess, with his blood money. But I had no way to know that."

"From the looks of things, the cull business is going to do well. I am considering buying the place we have for a ranch." He watched a velvet horned fat buck cross an open field.

"Have you looked at the bluestem country north of here?" she asked.

"No, is it as nice?"

"I was over it a few times with him on his business trips."

"Maybe I need to look more."

"We don't have to decide today, do we?"

"No," He leaned over and kissed her.

She laughed and he knew things were back on track for them

They were eating breakfast the next morning, when Marshal Cone and the boy, Willard Springer, arrived on horseback. Rath strapped on his six gun and he went out to meet them.

"I'll make more coffee for you men," she said from the back door.

They squatted down in the shade of her fruit bearing trees.

"I've been talking to Willard about what he knew about those men," Cone said. "He didn't know those two that were at the Highland Schoolhouse."

"You never met them anywhere?" Rath asked him.

"No, sir. But I figured they all lived over in the Pigeon Creek country."

Rath frowned. "Where's that?"

"East of the school house," Cone said. "Those men you wounded and Perry, the one got under the mule, were all from over there. So was Snowberry, who hired him."

"I never meant you no harm." The boy shook his head. "I sure never would have joined them."

"Thurman and Ferrell told me that some time ago. Who over there would hate me?"

"There's one old man over there that might fit that mold. He's a former commander of Kansas forces. In the war, you know, some of the outfits were federal and some local formed state outfits. This man was a Colonel Dixon and I heard they court marshaled him at the end of the war for what he did to some people who might have favored the south."

"Can we find him?" he asked Cone.

"That's not the problem. I think we need a posse. He might have some armed men to meet us."

"Everyone is busy around here, threshing wheat this week. I can get a few good men like Phillips, but they'd have to be back by Wednesday," Cone said.

"So we'd only have two days.' Squatted on the ground, Rath wondered who had said something about a Colonel? Where had he heard someone say they went to work for a Colonel Dixon? The bartender, Harry, said that Castrow had gone to work for some Colonel Dixon. Were they one and the same person? Who'd take revenge out on him and shoot his good horse? Costrow. His face to face meeting at the Crossing would have been on that sumbitch's mind if he rode with those night riders that night.

"What are you thinking about?" Cone asked.

"When I came up here last spring, I stopped at the Crossing and had a run-in with a Texas outlaw named Costrow. Had it not been for Harry, the bartender in the Texas Saloon, I might have been dead that day bucking three of them.

"Costrow left mad enough that day, I figure he shot my horse in the raid working for this Colonel."

"That's the best answer I ever heard. We can raise a posse and go question them. Is he wanted in Texas?"

Rath nodded. He'd bet good money that he was the one tried to bushwhack him coming home from the dance that night, too.

Cone agreed. "We can sure arrest him and hold him for the Texas authorities, if we can't tie him to the night riding."

"Can I go with you guys?" the boy asked.

"It might be dangerous," Cone said.

"I'd like to see my name cleared."

"If you'll stay back you can go along."

Cone swiveled on his toe around to talk to Rath. "When should we go up there?"

"I say be there at dawn. Catch them unaware. Who knows that area that good?" Rath asked.

"I'll find us someone today," Cone said.

"We'd need to leave here about midnight,"

"Alright I'll stop by and see if Phillips can ride with us too."

"That makes five of us,"

Cone nodded. "You still want to go along?" he asked Willard.

"Yes, sir."

"We'll meet here at midnight," Cone said,

They agreed and rose to shake hands. Rath saw his wife had the coffee ready. "Better have a cup."

"We wouldn't disappoint her," Cone said and removed his hat for her. "Sorry to bother your Sunday, ma'am."

"No problem, Marshal."

They introduced her to Willard and then went inside to sit at the kitchen table. When they finished, Rath saw them off. He watched the pair ride away and she joined him.

""What now?" She hugged his arm.

"We may have found the source of these night riders. Tonight, we're going to ride over there and surprise them at daylight and try to find some of them. I think a Texas outlaw may be one of them who I had a run in with coming up here."

"I hope that settles things. This use to be a nice place to live and we had no crimes. No robberies. No raids."

"I doubt it. The war left us with lots of criminal minded people, who lived by the gun then and continued to do so."

"You will be careful for me?"

"I will and myself too," He hugged her. If Costrow was in this plot to get him, there may be a good chance to stop him. The night he destroyed his wounded horse Reb returned to him like a bad dream.

"How are things going at the Crossing?" she asked.

"McDonald and I talked about buying more hay if we're going to keep all the cattle we have now. There is a stacker called a beaver board that piles hay way higher than you can reach and it can be moved to new sites. He's going to see if we can get two of them. There are lots of farmers willing to deliver us hay."

"You've been selling cows?"

"That's been going great. We will have them sold out, even the open ones, before fall. I really never counted on it working that well. Some investors want to buy some of the younger steers and grow them out. That might not be as big a profit center as the cows and the limper program, but it will help pay our costs. McDonald says his investors are really happy.

"We'll sell three hundred limbers in two weeks on the steer market and maybe sell some others to a few Indian agencies down in the Territory."

"Maybe you are an economist." She chuckled. "You remember to be careful tonight and tomorrow for me."

"I will, my love. I sure will."

Chapter18

Saddling his horse by lamplight, Rath recalled the old story they told about the Texas cowboys shooting so many holes in the sky that it was daylight at midnight in Abilene, Kansas. A million stars twinkled overhead when he came out of the house to get ready to ride. She stood nearby in the alleyway chewing on a long stem of hay and acting apprehensive about his leaving her on this mission.

"I keep wondering what I'd be doing not having you. My life from morning to night is like dancing in a field of wild flowers. That may sound silly to you, but you have taken a big weight off me."

"The Outlaw Queen anchor?"

She nodded. "Yes, that too. But it's you. You share yourself with me. You put up with my little-girl-like thinking at times."

"Those things appeal to me, they won't run me off."

"If you make lots of money, will you want to go back to Texas someday?"

"I don't think so. I really like Kansas. I think we can have a good life up here."

"I just wondered."

He turned his ear to listen. "I hear them coming. I'll be back tomorrow evening, or plan to be. If they run, I may have to pursue them."

She stood on her toes and kissed him. "I understand."

He gave her the lamp and led his gelding outside.

Cone was sitting a large powerful-built horse, Phillips had a good-looking saddle horse, Willard on a cowpony, and the last man was Slim Tagget. He shook Rath's hand. "Nice to meetcha. Glad to be along."

Tagget wore new bib overalls and a white shirt, but he rode a horse with ease. Might have been in the cavalry. They all rode a little straight backed.

Tagget led the way and they trotted most of the time. Their guide knew the country and wanted to take them in the back way to Colonel Dixon's place. They crossed some deep-cut creek banks and their horses had to scramble up the steep far side. Rath felt certain they was coming in the back side of things. But that might bar anyone from knowing about them coming.

They quietly surrounded the two-story farm house, saved by Willard coaxing the dogs and entertaining them. The house was dark. With his Winchester in hand, Rath set on his horse.

"Colonel Dixon, the law is here, sir. Come out with your hands in the air and if no one tries anything you all will live, but one peep and we will open fire."

Willard was standing back behind him. The swearing came next and the snarling. "Who in the hell is out there?"

Rath dried his hand on his pants and then cocked the Winchester. *The law is out here. How did they feel being surrounded?*

"What do you want?" a resident shouted at them.

"Everyone come out hands in the air or we'll shoot" The words weren't out of Cone's mouth when the back door rattled and a man in his underwear busted out and took the back steps three at a time.

"Halt!" Rath shouted.

Seeing the rifle pointed at his heart, the man threw up his hands and fell over backwards tripping the man on his heels and both fell in a pile. Tagget came rushing around and told Rath he had them. A third man came tearing out and ran left. He jumped off the porch and half jumped and then fell over the web wire yard fence on his face. On his feet again, he was bare footed and wearing a one piece underwear suit.

Rath bent over and ducked the top bar over the yard gate. He drove his pony in the open pasture after the fleeing subject. When he sent the gelding after him, he jammed the rifle in the scabbard then undid the *reata*. Running full-out and closing in on him, he shook loose a loop, swung it twice over his head, threw it over the runner's head and jerked the slack tight. The pony under him shut down and the runner screamed at being jerked backwards on his butt.

Out of the saddle, he had the familiar-faced outlaw by a handful of hair and drove a fist in his jawbone. "That's for shooting my horse."

Costrow laid on the ground and rubbed his jaw. "Damn shame I didn't have time to get all three, you bastard."

Filled with fury, Rath kicked him so hard in the side the man sprawled out on the ground groaning. Cone and Willard were there by then. Cone jumped off his horse to stop him, but Rath had quit by then.

Breathing and shuddering in his anger, wave and wave of madness went through him.

He straightened and took his hat from the boy with a nod. Then he began looping his *reata*. "He's the one shot Rebel." That said, he went for his horse. It was over. The sumbitch who had shot his good horse could face the judge and he could get on with his life with Mary Ann.

He stepped over to his horse then tied on his *reata*. "Who did you get at the house?"

"Snowberry, the Colonel, and a guy called Weeks."

"Think we've got them all?"

"If we don't, the others will run for fear we'll get them too."

He thanked the others, shook their hands and looked around. "You four can get them to jail. I've got a wife I need to go see. *Gracias, amigos.*"

Taking the main road, he short loped the roan horse for home. He'd need to find a few stout mares and start breeding himself some more good horses. He'd need them down the road for lots of things,

Hours later, in bed at his house with his wife, he stared at the board ceiling.

"What are you thinking now?" she asked on her elbows beside him.

"Where are these new ranches out here going to get cows to stock their ranges?"

"I wondered when you'd come up with that."

He half-raised and kissed her. "Shucks, there ain't much this ole cowboy and the outlaw queen of Kansas can't do, is there?"

"No, there sure isn't."

Dusty Richards is an author of numerous Western novels and a noted mentor each year to hundreds of beginning writers. Dusty

has won two Spur Awards, and a Heritage Award from the National Cowboy Museum in Oklahoma City. He has published more than 140 novels about the West.

Just a short list of some of the Dusty Richards' books you can find in the bookstore.

Texas
Waltzing with Tumbleweeds
Trail to Fort Smith
Deuces Wild
Wulf's Tracks
Texas Blood Feud
The Sundown Chaser
Montana Revenge
The Ogallala Trail
Trail to Cottonwood Falls
The Abilene Trail
Writing the West with Dusty Richards and Friends
Bounty Man and Doe
Cactus Country Anthology Volume I, II, & III

CPSIA information can be obtained at www.ICGtesting.com
Printed in the USA
LVOW04s1613250815

451473LV00025B/855/P